SMOKE AND RUIN

SMOKE AND RUIN

THE SIREN CHRONICLES BOOK THREE

TIFFANY DAUNE

Cover Design by Sefanie Saw (Seventhstar Art)

Blurb Copy by Carol Eastman

ISBN 9780995188181 (print) 9781777104245 (hardcover)
9780995188198 (ebook) 9781777104214 (ebook)

www.tiffanydaune.com

For my father who kept me grounded so I could fly.

1

Never remove a blade from a wound. Her mom's warning cried through the howling wind. Could her spirit see Halen now—read her frantic thoughts?

How else would her mom have known how desperately she wanted to let Dax sink to the ocean floor? He was a knife in her heart; if she let him go, death would follow.

Holding on tortured her worn muscles as she fought the waves from stealing his body from her grip. The unforgiving ocean shoved Dax forward, ramming his head into her jaw. Screaming, the salt water rushed between her lips, choking her breath. She was a siren—she wouldn't drown, but it didn't stop the ocean from trying to claim her.

She spewed out the brine as she shoved Dax back; not too far, just enough to hook her elbow through his. His limp body bobbed alongside hers, still unconscious since the moment their silver bracelets melded with their birthmarks. She feared any second now she may suffer the same listless fate.

Adjusting the water stone, she clutched the cylinder to her chest. This, too, she would gladly let slip into the ocean's depths if it weren't for the others. Her heart ached with the thought of Asair and Natalie. And how Asair's gaze flashed with rage when she wouldn't leave his side.

She had wanted to fight—her magick was stronger than his. But Galadia's wand required her protection.

Blinking the water from her eyes, she kicked toward the familiar shore. Dread swallowed her whole as her gaze drifted to her empty beach house. Rockaway was the last place she wanted to be, but where else could she go? At least here, Asair and Natalie might find her.

Her toes grazed the sandy bottom as a wave shoved her forward. She unhooked Dax, letting the next wave guide him to shore. She cast her gaze skyward as she made her way from the water. Clouds shrouded the moon, darkness her only friend.

As she dragged Dax from the ocean's grip, she scanned the vacant beach, thankful winter lingered on the Oregon coast. Summer would bring bonfires, late nights, and parties, but right now, the beach promised to keep her secrets safe.

She ran up a way, setting the water stone between the rocks. Even without sunlight, the crystal blue wand shimmered. A part of her wished she could leave it behind; she wished she had never set eyes on the cursed thing, and that someone else's past and future was tethered to Galadia's wand.

A wave rumbled along the shore. Her gaze darted to Dax, his body catching in the current.

"Oh, hell no!" She sprinted across the sand, hopping over a rock, bolting for the ocean before Dax drifted. "You're not getting away that easy." She heaved him to safety. Drained from the swim, exhausted from casting magick to push through the portal, she slowly dragged him toward the house. "Can you even hear me?" She yanked him and his head rolled to the side with no response.

She tilted him, being careful not to let his skull crack against the rocks, though the temptation to draw blood was great. His betrayal stung most. "I should leave you out here. It's what you deserve. Believe me, if those stupid bracelets hadn't melted under our skin, I would let the ocean eat you alive. I don't care what it would do to me."

She would welcome the pain of casting magick without the elixir remedy dragging her to the depths; face the fever, the puking, and even the nightmares if it severed the Guardian bond for good. Her birthmark glittered beneath the moonlight. A painful reminder separation wouldn't come that easy.

When she reached the garage doors, another wound stabbed her aching heart. She leaned into the doors as thoughts of her mom crushed around her. Her mom's warm smile, which had always brought her to a place of peace, flashed through her mind. Away from Asair, his magick, and the spell he had cast to mask her pain, her emotions flooded with sorrow. Halen had outrun grief, but now she was its captured prey.

Dax slipped from her grip, and she trembled, unable to go inside. She couldn't face this house alone. She glanced down at Dax. With his arms splayed at his sides, his skin a gray pallor, he could pass for a corpse. She sure as hell couldn't stay outside, either.

Swallowing back the rising tears, she punched in the alarm code. The double doors creaked open, stopping with a heavy thud. She scanned the street for signs of onlookers while she pulled Dax into the garage, ran back for the water stone, and hit the button, closing the doors. Her heart raced as she headed for the jar marked *nails* and scooped the key hidden within.

"Second chance key," she whispered as she envisioned her mom passing through the garage and dumping the jar of nails for the fifth time in a week, always leaving hers at the hospital. Halen held the key against her chest. She inhaled long and slow, trying to calm her rising tears.

Her hand shook, unable to place the key in the lock, as

if her body were fighting to let her enter, knowing once inside, she would succumb to the inevitable grief that awaited. But sorrow would follow no matter where she went. She opened the door.

The alarm sounded with steady, high-pitched beeps.

She punched in the code again, slamming the door, leaving Dax and the stone behind. Inside, loneliness nestled in her soul. She hugged herself tightly, staring at the bleak concrete walls as whispers of regret enveloped her.

You left them alone.

You should have fought.

You're weak.

You don't deserve the power.

Your mother is dead because of you.

With the tip of her toe, she skimmed the long fissures lining the concrete floors where she had cracked the ground when Ezra warned her about the Hunters. A lump swelled in her throat. He had sacrificed his life for Tage. Why couldn't Halen protect her friend?

You killed them too.

Murderer…

The weight of remorse dragged her to the cold, hard floor. She tucked her knees to her heaving chest. Why— why couldn't she have died instead? Sobbing into her soaking sleeves, she rolled to her side. She lay with her cheek pressed against the cracked concrete, wishing she could crawl inside and dig her way out of this hell.

2

WARM MORNING LIGHT spread across her battered body while the chill of grief blanketed Halen's soul. Memories flooded her mind, never letting her forget she had left Asair and Natalie behind; how she had searched for Dax and found him by the pond; how instead of fighting, she had shoved Dax in the water, dove in after him, and headed toward the open portal.

Coward, her thoughts screamed.

And she agreed. She had the water stone; she had more power than Asair or her sister, yet she was the one who ran. Her magick saved her from the clawing ocean, not strength. But now she was paying for having depended on her sparks to bring her home.

She rubbed her throbbing head. Every cell ached as if she was splitting apart from the inside out. Her eyelids grew heavy at the thought of staying awake. Already, fever pinched her skin, nausea not far behind. This was the price of casting magick.

She groaned, staring at the steps, seeming miles high, but her salvation sat upstairs in her mom's medicine cabinet. At least she hoped the coral and bone elixir was still there.

Rising, her damp clothes clung to her body; the sand

5

crumbling off like a winter molt. Leaning against the wall for support, she lifted her foot onto the first stair.

Her silver birthmark glittered in the sun beaming from the skylights. The reflected rays bounced along the walls, almost beautiful if it weren't for the gruesome reminder that she was permanently tied to the douchebag in the garage.

Her stomach roiled with the thought. Slapping her hand over her mouth, she sprinted, reaching the spare bathroom before hurling. She swiped her mouth clean with the hand towel and ran the tap, sipping the cool water from the faucet. She met her battered reflection. "Who the hell are you?" The words croaked from her throat.

Sand matted her hair, scratches lined her face, and a purple bruise formed along her jaw where Dax's head had rammed into her. Her shirt was stained not from her blood, but her sister's. She clutched the sides of the sink as the image of an arrow stuck fast in Natalie's back haunted her thoughts. She inhaled a deep breath through her nose and out through her mouth, keeping the next wave of vomit at bay.

She crossed the hall and into her mom's bedroom. As she passed her bed, the vanilla scent of her perfume hit Halen like the death blow in a knockout fight. She gasped, choking back the tears, as she made her way to the on-suite bathroom. When she pried open the cabinet, she spotted a single vial of elixir on the shelf. Not enough coral and bone to cast much magick, but enough to stabilize her nerves until she figured out her next step.

She tilted back the vial; the sticky sweet concoction passed her lips, slipping down her throat, and her flesh warmed with sparks trailing along her arms. She peeled off her clothes and placed them in the hamper. Ripped and bloodstained, they were past cleaning, but the habit made her feel a little less out of control.

Shivering, she flicked on the tub faucet. While the basin filled, she searched the drawers for more vials her mom may have stashed away. Finding nothing, she slipped on her robe and headed into the bedroom. Her breath hitched. Everything was as she had left it; her teacup beside the bed, her book downturned and opened to the last page she'd read.

She perched on the edge of the bed, grabbing her mom's pillow up in her arms. Halen buried her face in the plush down while grief tore at her broken heart like a starved beast.

"Mom, I'm so sorry," she screamed into the pillow. She rubbed her cheek across the soft cotton. "I messed everything up."

Tarius lives, her mom's voice whispered past her ear. *You must stay strong.*

"Mom?" Halen stood. "Are you there?" Her heart slammed in her chest. "Mom!"

A chain of little beeps drew her attention to the desk. Her mom's laptop illuminated with a picture of their smiling faces.

They stood beneath the shade of an oak tree, clover at their feet. The sun poked through the canopy of leaves, highlighting her mom's deep auburn hair with coppery speckles. Halen grasped the sides of the laptop, wanting desperately to transport to that moment, to have her mom close, hold her, and never let her go. She never should have left her in that hotel room surrounded by the Hunters. But she hadn't meant to leave.

"Dax." She hissed between gritted teeth. Dax had scooped her in his arms and dived through the portal. Her death was his fault, too.

Halen scrolled through the last photo album they had made together, a montage of cities where they had lived.

Beside the album, a folder labeled *Our Special Places* tugged her curiosity.

"What's this?" Had her mom started an album on her own? When she clicked on the folder, a single image filled the screen. The foreboding sculpture sparked her magick at once. The onyx angel marked the entrance to their rocky garden, a monument to her father. Its bleek gaze peered toward the ocean set on the spot where Huron had battled the waves.

"What? This isn't a *special place*. He's not even dead." Halen shook the sparks from her fingertips, which rose so easily with the thought of her father. "I don't understand. Mom, if you're there, please show me."

The patter of water slapping the tile floor answered instead. "Oh no!" Jumping up, she ran into the bathroom and flicked the faucet off.

A crash boomed from downstairs and her sparks electrified across her chest. Had she forgotten to set the alarm? She tightened the belt along her robe as she tiptoed into the hall.

"Hello?" She peered down the stairs.

Thump thump thump.

She slapped her hand over her mouth to stifle her scream.

Another *thump* and then a low howl carried from the garage. Was Dax awake?

She ran down the stairs two at a time. At the door, she pressed her ear against the cool metal. The crash of glass shattering on concrete stole her breath. She jumped back, her heart beating wild against her chest.

Would Dax harm her? Or would he leave and find the Tari? If he took off, she wouldn't have his marrow. Magick would be out of the question, and she might need a hell of a lot to find Asair and her sister. She couldn't let him escape.

8

Slowly, she cracked open the door, her other hand pressed against the air, preparing to strike when the door jammed. Her pulse raced as something brushed her feet. She swung downward, ready to unleash her sparks. But she stopped midair.

A calico cat peered up and meowed.

"Spinnaker! What the heck are you doing here?"

He purred, nuzzling her ankles with the top of his head.

"You stupid cat." She scooped him up. "I almost fried you." As if sensing the truth of her words, he wriggled from her arms. She pushed back the door, only to find Dax blocking the way. Spinnaker licked the ocean salt from his forehead.

"Did I let you in?"

Spinnaker meowed.

"Come on, then." She opened the side door, the cool morning air slipping inside. "Go on, before your mom comes searching for you." The last thing she needed was her neighbor nosing around.

Spinnaker protested, rolling on the garage floor.

Halen sighed, picking him up. "Sorry, buddy, but your mom will freak if you're missing." She tossed him outside and secured the deadbolt. Leaning with her back against the door, she stared at the unconscious boy. His damp clothes clung to his body, his skin flecked with goosebumps. "I guess I better take you inside."

Tired, the thought of moving him with magick crossed her mind, but with only one bottle of elixir to her name, she needed to conserve. "Come on, you big lump." Lifting Dax under his arms, she dragged him into the living room and switched on the gas fireplace.

Though the flames cast a soft glow over his listless body, his lips remained a purplish-blue hue. She winced, thinking how his kiss had once ignited a fire beneath her skin, laced through her magick, and held on tightly like strangling reigns. So many lies had passed through those lips. Sparks swelled with her anger. "I'm not wasting my magick on you." She pumped her fists, releasing the energy.

He didn't deserve comfort, but she had to keep him alive. So, instead of letting him freeze, she stripped off his wet clothes and covered him with a blanket. Her gaze drifted to his matching birthmark, the silver sparkling on his skin. If she stayed close to him, would the bond capture her heart as Asair had warned?

She feared loving Dax. She feared killing him. But most of all, his control over her power terrified her the most. And what it might take to break the bond—death.

Trailing her fingers across the swirl at his shoulder, the silver rippled beneath his skin. She flinched back as the silver transformed into a single circle. Her arm burned with fiery pain. Crying out, she grasped her shoulder. Craning her neck, she witnessed the silver beneath her skin mimic Dax's mark. "What the hell?" She touched the newly formed circle.

She peeked beneath the blanket. His birthmark along his lower arm remained unchanged. A sick feeling twisted her gut as a horrible thought crept into her mind. What if there wasn't a way to set Dax free? What if they were bound forever?

No. She shook the horrible thought away. There had to be a way out. She wouldn't live with the fear of this monster lurking along the seam of her soul, manipulating her magick.

Her thoughts raced with a new idea. Halen charged through the living room and into the kitchen. She flung open the knife drawer. The steel blades glistened like the silvery curse beneath her skin. Choosing the sharpest one, she ran the tip along her forearm. With her shaking fist, she poked at the little starburst pattern, wedging the blade below the inner swirl. Crimson washed over the Guardian stain, reminding her of the river of blood that plagued her thoughts—the boy and stag, waiting. Dax would gladly deliver her to Tarius. She wouldn't let him try. She winced as she dug the blade farther.

This is not the way, her mom's soft voice whispered at her back.

She dropped the knife at once. Grabbing the dishtowel, she applied pressure to the wound. What did it matter? One little spot wouldn't make a difference; she would have to cut off her entire arm if she wanted to be free.

Tears welled in her eyes and she wiped them away. The kitchen shifted in her focus. Her breath shallowed as an inexplicable force wound through her. She blinked, grasping the counter for support as the pull tugged her toward the boy on the other side of the door.

"What the hell?" She all but found her steps leading to Dax, even though she had wanted to stay in the kitchen.

His forehead beaded with fever, and a wave of chills spread along her skin. She pressed her damp head to her sleeve, noticing the heat of her cheeks. She glanced in the mirror, finding her skin, too, was flushed with fever. "This is so not happening."

She rushed to the kitchen, shoving her wrists beneath the cool tap water, but the fever spread. Her teeth chattered as she wet a dishcloth and filled a bowl with ice. Hurrying back to Dax, she draped the cloth across his head and placed the ice over his skin.

"Are you trying to kill us?" she asked but realized the answer was more complicated than that. If they were this connected, she had to make sure he lived.

She headed to the hall closet where her mom kept some of Huron's old clothing. When she brought the box down from the shelf, his salty scent filled the air. This had been a smell she had loved as a child; how it lingered in his hair and on her pillow long after he left after telling her stories about the sea. Now the brine turned her stomach.

As she carried the box to the living room, she wondered where her creep of a father might be lurking. With Tarius still locked away, it was only a matter of time before Huron came for the stone—before he sought revenge. It sickened her, knowing her father loved a demon more than his daughters. That he would sacrifice her for power.

Setting the box beside Dax, she dug through the clothes and found a long-sleeved blue cotton shirt, which would match his eyes perfectly if they ever opened. She tested his forehead once more. Sparks danced up her wrist to the crook of her elbow and she pulled back, hating the way the Guardian bond manipulated her magick.

She finished dressing him quickly, being careful to limit skin-to-skin contact. How the heck was she supposed to tend to Dax while searching for her sister and Asair? She couldn't just leave him behind, nor could she travel with him. The Guardian bond had screwed her royally.

A gust of wind pushed against the windows. She jumped when the patio door flew open with a *whish* of a breeze. Her magick flickered. Halen scanned the empty beach beyond, searching the shadows and between the waves. Her gaze drifted to the stone angel from her mother's pictures. *Our Special Places.* The album name tugged her curiosity once more. Drawn to the angel, she approached the open door. Winter winds whistled in her ears, warning her not to go outside, but her gut wound with a feeling there was something she needed to see.

Keeping a watchful eye on the beach, she made her way along the pebbled path to the angel. Standing before the onyx sculpture, shivers ran down her spine; its glazed stare stirring memories of the Hunter Lina transformed to

12

stone. She crouched by the angel's feet, where she had spent many days sketching beneath the shadow of stone wings, mourning for a father who hadn't even died.

She caught the flickering sound of something catching in the wind; a piece of plastic tucked beneath the podium. The surrounding sand mounded on one side, revealing evidence of a recently dug hole.

When she nudged the statue, it rocked in her grip. "Hmmm…" Pushing with both hands, the angel tipped, clipping its wing on the rocks as it fell. She yanked the corner of the plastic bag, freeing it from the sand. Her sparks tripped when she spread open the seal.

Reaching inside, she pulled out a letter. A coffee ring stained the envelope, its contents weighted. The wind shoved against her, tossing sand in her eyes as if nature were fighting her for the contents. She tucked the envelope to her chest and ran back inside, slamming the door behind her.

Halen tore open the envelope, and a key dropped to her feet, pinging on the concrete. She picked it up, clutching the cool metal in her fist as she unfolded the letter. Scrawled on the page, she found her mom's handwriting, big in some places and then minuscule as she crammed in the last few words. *I love you always.*

Her hands shook as she read the letter in its entirety.

My dearest daughter,

If you're reading this, then everything went horribly wrong. You must be so scared. And I'm so sorry I can't be there with you. I know it may seem impossible, but you must stay strong. I want you to know that I chose this life. The decisions I made were mine. Whatever the consequences, they lie with me alone. A life of secrets catches up to you.

Listen to your heart. Don't follow blindly. Be brave.

The key is for Sarah Winters at the bank. She has everything you need.

I love you always,
Mom

Curiosity spun with fear as Halen opened her trembling hand, revealing the simple brass key. None of this made sense. Why go to so much trouble to hide this key? She couldn't share a secret like hers with just anyone. Who in the world was Sarah Winters?

3

SLIDING the brim of her ball cap down, Halen peered
inside the bank window. With a bruised jaw combined with
a rash of nicks and scrapes, she looked more like a fugitive
than a customer. She needed to find Sarah Winters and
fast before she drew attention. Inhaling a deep breath, she
summoned the courage and entered the bank.

Fluorescent lights buzzed above; a baby screamed in a
stroller; a man broke out in a fit of sneezing, making her
jump. Her stomach knotted, and she glanced toward the
exit.

Stay strong, her mom's whispered voice urged.

She tucked her hands into her down parka, turning the
key in her pocket, rolling it between her fingers as she fell
in line behind an elderly lady. The woman's patchouli-
scented scarf stirred memories of Jae's home where Halen
had purged Asair. She had wanted nothing more than to
be free of him. Now, if she found him, she would never let
him go.

"Miss, I can help you here." A young man with hair
the color of autumn leaves waved her forward. As she
approached the counter, she turned when the security
camera panned her way. She adjusted her collar, pulling it
up high. The Tari used satellite imagery to track the fires;
facial recognition wasn't out of their grasp. Even with the

aqueducts destroyed, Halen figured they had more than one base. She feared they had eyes on her now. With sweaty palms, she straightened the plaque with the name *Peter* engraved across the front.

"How may I help you today?" His face beamed with a broad customer service smile. He wore a button down, oxford shirt with the sleeves rolled at the hem, and a neat bowtie affixed at his neck, which matched his green rimmed glasses. As pleasant as he seemed, this wasn't who she needed.

She glanced at the woman beside him, searching for Sarah Winters's name, but her plaque read *Alicia*. Either Sarah wasn't working today, or she held another position. Pulling the key out of her pocket, she set it on the counter and formed a protective cage over the top with her fingers. "I was hoping to speak with Sarah Winters?"

Peter's face flushed bright red. His gaze fell to the three dots on her hand; her birthmark was now a dull silver beneath the artificial lighting.

"Is she here?" Halen clasped the key.

"How do you know Sarah?" His gaze remained fixed on her hand. At the mention of her name, Alicia peered over.

Halen's sparks flickered. Scooping the key, she slipped her hands back in her pockets. This was a bad idea. She should have just called.

A muscular man stuffed in a suit two sizes too small stepped behind Peter. "Is there a problem?"

Peter let out a soft whimper as he wiped away a tear.

What had she said? Halen turned to leave when Alicia answered him, "She's here to see Sarah." Halen shot the snitch a pointed stare.

The man placed his hand on Peter's shoulder, excusing him. "I'll handle this. Miss, do you mind joining me at my desk?"

Heck yes, I mind. An uneasy feeling crept through her as more tears rimmed Peter's eyes.

"I've got this." Alicia placed the closed sign at his wicket. "Take your break."

The man nodded to his left.

Halen glanced toward the door. She should make a run for it, but her mom had gone through the trouble of hiding the key and the note... Why, then, did her sparks flicker as if she was entering a trap? Yet, when the man opened the gate, she walked through.

"I'm Gordon Monroe. I'm the bank manager." He took a seat behind his desk. "Sorry about that. Peter was close to Miss Winters."

"*Was* close?" Halen's voice cracked.

He leaned back, crossing his arms. "You're Corinne's daughter? Please have a seat."

"How did you know?" As she sat, she glanced over her shoulder at the exit once more. *Run,* her thoughts urged.

"Your picture was on my desk."

"Excuse me?"

"In the newspaper." His eyebrows rose. When she didn't respond, he continued. "Your mom was glowing when you won the swim tournament. She couldn't stop looking at the paper on my desk. I haven't seen her in here for a while, and that other man she's always with... what's his name—Daspar? What kind of name is that anyway—Daspar?" He sighed, shaking his head.

She wriggled in her seat, prepared to bolt. If this guy knew her mom so well, why didn't she send her to meet him instead of this Sarah Winters? She met his beady, black stare. Something was off.

An office door closed, sending the scent of damp fur swirling into the air. She sniffed, her gaze sharp on Monroe. He had an odd sort of way about him, but a shifter working as a bank a manager? Again, the distinct musty scent of fur drifted past her nose. She stood, clutching the key. "I'm sorry. I think there's been a mistake." She didn't even wait for him to speak as she pushed past the gate and rushed out the front door.

Outside, she bent with her hands on her knees. Her pulse raced as she steadied the rising sparks. *Damn it!* Why did everything have to be so hard? Why couldn't just one thing fall into place? Just one freaking time.

Was that so much to ask? Now how would she find Sarah Winters? She couldn't just go back in, not after acting like such a spaz. Not if the bank manager *was* a shifter. Monroe could easily be on the Tari's side. "Why here, Mom?" She cast her gaze toward the heavens, shaking her head.

As she turned to cross the street, the heavy scent of cinnamon drew her attention. She spotted Peter in the alley, leaning against the brick building, a vapor cloud curling into the cool air. She should leave him alone after how he had reacted when she mentioned Sarah, but she didn't see another choice. He at least knew Sarah.

She stopped in front of him. "Hi, I'm sorry about all that in the bank. I didn't know..." She hoped he would fill in the blanks.

"Yeah, no, it's my fault." He inhaled a long drag of his e-cigarette. "I can't believe she's gone." The vapor hitched in his breath. He exhaled, coughing into his sleeve. "I didn't mean to freak out on you."

"She's gone?"

His gaze dropped to her hand once more. "Who are you?"

She tucked her hand up in her sleeve. "Halen Windspeare. My mom banks here." She kept her conversation in the present tense, omitting the part about her being dead. She didn't quite think Peter needed all the details. "She asked me to meet with Sarah."

His brow furrowed. "Then you haven't heard the news?"

She shook her head. "We've been out of town. I just got back."

He sucked the tip of his e-cigarette, inhaling deeply.

"She's dead."

"What?" Her sparks surged.

He exhaled, enveloping them in a cloud of cinnamon and dread. "Some kids found her body on the beach. She drowned." Again, his attention drifted to her wrist.

"I'm sorry," Halen said, not sure how to continue. Yes, this was tragic news, but she needed to figure out what the key was for. If he had been friends with Sarah, maybe he knew more. She took the key out of her pocket, holding it out for him to see. "Do you know what this might be for?"

He shrugged.

"Are you sure?" She pushed her hand toward him, her bare wrist shimmering in the sunlight.

He grabbed her arm, shoving up her sleeve. His eyes widened. "Sarah had a mark like this, too. Only it wasn't silver. Are you in some kind of cult?" His grip tightened.

Halen yanked hard, breaking free. She shoved her sleeve down. "No! I mean yes. We were both abducted in this messed up cult when we were kids." The lies rushed out all at once. "They tattooed these marks on us." Her story wasn't legitimate, but his story was even more unbelievable; if Sarah Winters had a siren birthmark, she sure as heck didn't drown.

His eyes pooled with concern. "Oh man, I had no idea. Sarah never said anything. That makes sense why she always hid the marks. She wouldn't even let me see them when we were…" His voice trailed off as the tears welled once more.

Halen touched his sleeve. "Sarah had something for me. I think the cult may be after me." The Tari wasn't

19

exactly a cult, neither were the shifters, but the Hunters, on the other hand... They lived for one purpose, compelled by a curse to capture siren souls. They must have found Sarah and used her soul to build up strength for the fight in the forest. Her fists clenched. Natalie was a fool to trust them. "I really need to know what the key is for."

"Show me again." He nodded toward her pocket.

Halen pulled the key out and handed it to him.

He turned it over, examining the engraved numbers. "It's a key to the new storage lockers at the Shorewood RV Park. Sarah's dad spends his summers there. *Did* spend his summers there." He sniffed back the next wave of emerging tears.

She had pushed too far, but she couldn't stop now. "I know this is hard, but I need your help. The key is for a locker?"

"I can take you there if you'd like. I know where Sarah kept his things. It's all just a bunch of old fishing gear, though. She wouldn't keep anything valuable there."

"I need to see for myself."

"I'll show you the locker. I've got the access code to the building written down at home."

She wasn't catching any bad vibes from Peter. He seemed genuinely hurt and now concerned for her as well. She shouldn't have fibbed, but what choice did she have? "That would be great."

"I get off at five. Do you want me to pick you up?"

"No, I can ride my bike. It's not too far from my house."

"Be careful." Peter's gaze drifted to her wrist.

She nodded, knowing full well she could obliterate anyone who came near her. The problem was that she didn't have much elixir. Hopefully, she wouldn't need magick before five. "See you later." She ran across the street, glancing back as Peter disappeared into the bank.

Would Monroe stop him? Did she even need to worry about the bank manager? He hadn't actually threatened her. If he were a shifter, then he would have followed. No, it was just paranoia screwing with her mind. But as she hopped on her bike, she realized some of her frantic thoughts might be warranted. If the portal brought her to Rockaway, others may have followed. The Hunters could be in Rockaway this very minute.

Her sparks pricked with the thought, and she peddled faster. Adding to her panic, the only person her mom trusted with their secret was dead. Sitting at the beach house until five was a risk. She only hoped whatever her mom had given Sarah was worth the wait.

HALEN RUSHED to check on Dax. As much as she hated him, a gold arrow would be a death sentence for both of them. If she didn't have magick to fight, then all would be lost. Like a lion protecting its kill from the rest of the hungry pack, she dragged him through the kitchen into the laundry room. When she tucked a towel under his head, he released a rushed breath.

She jumped back. "Dax? Are you awake?" She poked him with the tip of her sneaker, but he didn't budge. "Can you hear me?" She nudged harder, but he lay still as stone. "Well, just in case you wake up, I can't have you roaming around." She shut the laundry room door, then wedged a chair up against the handle. She had seen this trick in a movie but had no clue if it worked. So, just to be sure, she slid over all three bar stools, creating a barricade against the door. Her fortress might contain Dax, but it wouldn't protect him from the Hunters.

"Ugh. Why did you trust them, Nat?" She couldn't believe her sister banded with killers. "What kind of lies did they feed you?" A terrible thought crossed her mind. What if Asair and Natalie had died at the hands of the Hunters, too? No. She shook her head. She couldn't think this way. Jae would have protected them. She was a powerful dragon. But how would they find her if she was on the run?

Halen checked the oven clock; too long until she met with Peter. She could blow the storage locker door open with magick, but if the Hunters were already in Rockaway, then it would draw them right to her. She had no choice but to wait.

She headed upstairs to her mom's room, where she opened the computer, hoping she had left more clues. Scanning the pictures, tears choked her when she stopped on one. Halen remembered this day well; her father was supposed to visit, but of course, he was a no-show. But her mom, like always, had made the best of the day. They had folded newspaper pages into little boats to float down the canal until the night sky had bloomed with stars. Her mom had pointed out the Big Dipper and the Little Dipper while their paper armadas floated out to sea. It had been a simple day—a day she would give anything to repeat.

She checked the time again. Peter wouldn't be off yet. "It doesn't hurt to be early." She headed down the stairs. Besides, she could scope out the RV park before Peter arrived. If Hunters were in the area, then she wouldn't allow Peter to be caught in the crossfire. He had suffered enough.

Halen slid on her parka and tucked the elixir in her pocket, just in case. She should take the coral and bone beforehand, but she didn't want to waste a single drop if a threat didn't present itself. She double-checked the stool barricade, leaned her ear to the door to listen for movement, and when all seemed well, she set the alarm and headed out. Checking both ways, she searched for signs of Hunters. Not that they would hide. There was nothing subtle about the pack of immortals. If they were here, she would know, or she would be dead already.

SHE INHALED THE CRISP, salt air as the wind brushed her face. The ocean called to her, begging her to come out and play. Being this close to the water—to the driving force of her magick—twisted her inside out. Before the mermaids, before Elosia and the water stone, the ocean simply beat the shore, but now its energy thundered in her chest, rolling with the rhythm of her heart. The last time she traveled down these streets, she was simply Halen Windspeare: messed up student, freak who blacked out in class, girl who sketched the sea. Not that she ever felt normal. But at least she had thought that she was human, that whatever had caused all the horrible things around her to happen, there had been a scientific reason, a cure.

She passed through the gates of the RV park and rested her bike against the new building. Standing beneath the lamp post, she removed the key from her pocket, but the shiny keypad blocked her from entering. Her fingertips enlivened with sparks, daring her to enter on her own. "I can't," she said out loud and laughed at the ridiculousness of talking to her magick. It didn't have a life of its own; it was she who was in control.

And Dax.

He, too, had a magick pass. She wouldn't soon forget how his anger had spun her sparks into a spear to launch at Rania. And how she had retaliated with her mutant army. She couldn't allow him access again. But then again, she didn't know if she had a choice. Hopefully, whatever her mom had left would help her find a way out of this mess. She leaned against the building, tucking her arms around her while scanning the empty RV slips. Tree branches swayed with the rising winds, casting shadows along the concrete and stirring her already frazzled nerves. She hugged herself tighter.

A car entered, and the driver flashed their high beams.

She shielded her eyes as the car parked in the space across from her.

When the purr of the engine died, Peter hopped out and waved. "Hi, looks like it's a good thing I'm early. The boss sent me home after what happened today. He's making me take a few days off."

"I'm really sorry." Poor guy. Visiting his dead girl-friend's storage locker was probably the last place he wanted to be. Yet here he was after a stressful day at work to help her out. Peter was a rock star in her books.

"Hey, it's not your fault. He's probably right, anyway. I should have taken the time off before." He stood by the keypad, removing a crumpled piece of paper from his pocket, and punched in a code. "Well, let's see what Sarah had for you." The door buzzed when he entered the last digit and yanked it open. "After you." He waved her forward.

Metal-caged lights hung overhead; when Peter flipped the switch, they hummed to life. Halen glanced down the narrow hallway filled with storage lockers. Musty lifejack-ets, fishing poles, crab traps, and coolers filled the wire lockers. Halen hoped her mom's idea of survival gear wasn't quite so *survival-y*. She wasn't much of a camper. She peered in a locker filled with colorful kites, then made her way to the next one.

"Over here!" Peter's voice boomed in the hollows of the building. "It's up there." He pointed to the locker above. "Her dad didn't have much to store." He grabbed a ladder and placed it against the bottom locker. "I can go up if you like."

Her mom had gone to great lengths to hide the key and entrust it with only one person. She had to open the locker. "I've got this."

She took one step up but stopped as the pungent scent

of damp fur wafted past her nose. *Monroe.* She sniffed the air, turning back toward Peter. "Were you followed?"

The ping of metal hitting concrete echoed from the next aisle. Sparks trailed her arms.

Peter brought his finger to his lips, motioning for her to be quiet. "I'll check it out." He whispered, glancing nervously over the rims of his glasses.

"I'll go." She snagged his jacket sleeve. No way would she let him get hurt.

A *swoosh* followed by a rustling shoved her siren senses into overdrive. "Stay here." She held her hand against the air. Halen crept toward the end of the aisle. She felt life on the other side; their shallow breath competing with her rapid heartbeat pounding against her rib cage. Sparks charged along her skin. She rolled her shoulders back, prepared to fight, and stepped into the open.

Her breath hitched when she caught sight of a man. Sand coated his feet, water beaded his muscled chest, and his wide, crystal-clear Elosian eyes cut through her.

"How lucky can I be?" A sly grin played on his lips. "You're the one, aren't you?"

Halen inched back when her shoulders bumped into something hard. Peter's warm breath fell at her neck. As she reached to push him away from danger, he grabbed her arm.

The Elosian man's grin broadened. "Hello, Peter."

Panic ran like a screaming banshee through Halen. She glanced back at Peter and then to the Elosian. Peter's fist clamped tighter. "What are you doing?" Her voice cracked with fear.

"Sarah told me everything before she died. Of course, it took some persuasion." His nails dug into her flesh. "I've been waiting for you."

"Who are you?" Her gaze met with the Elosian. "Did my father send you?"

He laughed, shaking the water from his blond hair. "We're done with your father's games. Rania has promised great rewards for any siren head, but for yours…" His brows quirked up over gleaming eyes. "With you, I will secure a position on the council."

"If you kill me, the portal will open. Tarius will be free. Surely, Rania doesn't want to set a demon loose?"

"The portal won't open. We're taking you to the Hunters. Your soul will remain safe in their arrows while we eradicate the rest of the sirens."

"Rania is not who she seems." She shoved hard against Peter, but he was much stronger than he appeared. Again, she caught a whiff of damp fur. Was Monroe lurking in the shadows, too? Her sparks heated. "Her son was a siren. Did she tell you?"

"And she paid the price for her sin." Reaching for the strap at his waist, he pulled out a dagger; the blade hooked like a sickle, and the metal shone with encrusted diamonds.

A knife? Was he serious? Even with all that bling, he might as well be brandishing a toothpick. She could handle a simple blade.

The Elosian lunged.

Peter shoved her forward, and the blade nicked her palm, sending a fiery pain across her skin. She screamed out as her blood dripped, sizzling on the concrete. "What did you do?" Her gaze darted to the dagger, before landing on the man's satisfied stare.

"Come with me and I won't need to show you the extent of its powers." The Elosian aimed the weapon, ready to strike. "There's no need to suffer. I've heard you're a nice girl."

"You heard wrong." With a flick of her wrist, she unleashed a jolt of electricity through the Elosian. He flew back against the door, flinging it open.

The ocean winds whipped through the building, howling with a hollow moan.

"Sarah fought too." Before her eyes, Peter dropped to the ground, falling in what seemed like slow motion as his transition happened so fast, yet so clearly. His shoulders rounded with bristling striped fur; his hands and feet formed padded paws with razor-pointed claws. Whiskers sprouted from his cheeks, his jaw lengthened, his eyes narrowed, and his whole body twisted and shifted until she found herself face-to-face with a beast.

Halen's breath caught. The scent at the bank hadn't belonged to Monroe. "You're Etlin?"

The tiger released a thunderous roar.

"You can't kill this one." The Elosian narrowed the space between them.

Pressed between a blood-boiling dagger and sharp incisors, her magick surged. She struck the tiger first, shoving him away, but he shook away her magick and widened his stance.

The ocean breeze called to her magick, now charging along her skin. She searched the static energy within the wind, beckoning it to her command with a clap of her hands.

The tiger sprang, but she whipped the winds around the feline, drawing him toward the ceiling. He struggled in her grasp, and she fought to hold on. He roared with his rage, and this, too, called to her sparks. She wound the wind like rope harnessing the energy within; the bindings crisscrossed, digging into his fur. He thrashed against her wind cage, snarling with a fierce growl.

The Elosian darted for the open door and her sparks enlivened with a new, twisted energy, one that craved revenge.

Let him go. Her mother's voice rang through her mind.

Kill him. Dax's voice sang louder.

28

She flinched at the sound of his voice.

If you let him go, others will follow. Dax coaxed her magick to her hands. Curling her fingers inward, she slammed the door shut before the Elosian crossed the threshold.

"Please!" He pounded on the metal door.

With a wave of her hand, she captured his weapon; the blade hung in midair, the tip aimed at his muscled chest. His frantic heartbeat called to her from the dark side of her seam.

Do it, Dax whispered.

Traveling in unchartered waters with Dax at the helm, she couldn't resist the temptation—she didn't even try.

With the tip of the blade, she drew the metal across his chest. Blood bubbled from his skin. He wailed with agony and his cries fueled her sparks. With a flick of her fingers, she thrust him back and continued carving her message.

"Please, let me go." Tears rolled down his cheeks.

The tiger roared, igniting a fresh wave of sparks. Shaking her fist, the bindings tightened. The tiger pawed the wind ropes, trying to shred his way out. Her force was stronger. She clenched her fist tight, her nails digging into her flesh, but she did not stop until the tiger was silenced.

This is not the way. The whispered voice of her mom swarmed her.

"They'll kill me." Halen swatted her voice away. "Death is the only way."

Her mother's voice persisted. *Tarius craves rage—resist.*

Her gaze darted to the Elosian. Blood tears dripped down his cheeks as he squirmed beneath the poised dagger.

You are stronger than this. Remember who you are.

Halen's chest ached with her words. She released her fist at once. The tiger plunged to the concrete, his coppery stare void of life. She knelt, grabbing his fur in her fists.

"What have I done?" Her thoughts flashed with Dax, a

rifle propped on his shoulder, aimed at Wolfe. She drew back, inhaling sharply. Had he captured her magick?

"You're all demons," the Elosian shouted.

How could she argue otherwise with a dead shifter at her feet? She blew out, releasing the last of her sparks, and the door flew open.

The Elosian bolted. The bloodied dagger dropped, landing with a ringing clang. Choking back the regret, she tore her gaze from the dead shifter and studied her hands, which were now a blackish-blue tinge from the dark magick she had cast. Her head grew light, swimming with Peter's death and how easily her magick had stolen his breath.

She glanced once more at the boy whose life she had taken. She couldn't just leave him, but she didn't have time to move him, either. The look of disdain in the Elosian man's eyes meant he would return—and not alone. Despite her remorse, the need to survive was stronger. She had to collect whatever Sarah Winters hid for her and get the hell out before more trouble arrived.

She ran, stopping at the locker. As she grasped the ladder, her hands shook, her feet unable to lift to the first step. She fumbled, unscrewing the vial of elixir from her pocket. She downed the coral and bone, sipping every drop until her sparks awakened. Though thankful for the boost, this energy scared her. If more Elosians arrived, would the darkness drive her to kill them, too? Her unconscious Guardian had too much control. She needed to get home and get the hell out of Rockaway before anyone else got hurt.

Using her mom's key, she unfastened the lock and opened the locker door. Her heart sank. Life jackets and fishing rods mocked her; nothing but a bunch of junk. Halen pinched her eyes tightly as a sharp pain cut across her temple. Her mom's gift had to be somewhere in all this mess—she needed it to be. Digging past the life jackets, she spotted a beat-up cooler; the lid sat askew, the plug missing. As she chucked the cooler aside, it seemed oddly heavy. Prying the lid open, she peeked inside. Her jaw dropped.

She pulled out a thick stack of bills. Several more bands of money lined the inside. Had Sarah and her dad robbed a bank? Thinking that this was not what her mom had left behind for her, she was about to push the cooler aside when a shimmer drew her attention. Beneath the bills, a long wooden box with a shiny brass clasp called to her. When she popped open the box, a smile filled her face. Eighteen vials of elixir lay cradled in royal blue velvet. "Thank you, mom," she whispered under her breath.

Stuffing the money in her pockets, she scanned the locker once more to make certain she hadn't missed anything. With the box tucked under her arm, Halen descended the ladder while keeping an ear out for signs of others. She paused at the door, guilt dragging her thoughts back to Peter. "I'm sorry," she said and pushed through into the chill of the night.

A seagull landed on the lamp post, releasing a high-pitched cry. The bird's stare followed as she made her way to her bike. *Not every animal is a shifter.* She shook away the sparks rising with her fear.

She hopped on the bicycle, setting the box of elixir in the basket. As she peddled alongside the ocean, she scanned the shadows and waves. With the coral and bone coursing through her veins, she could fight… But for how long? And at what price? She glanced toward the wooden box. A part of her urged her to throw the elixir away, quell the sparks before she killed again, but the other half of her knew there would never be an escape.

5

Even with the doors bolted and the alarm set, Halen's sparks remained ready to strike. She felt electric as if someone could combust with her touch. She held her blue-tinged palms to the light. What had she done? What if the Elosian were right—what if the earth was safer with her soul locked eternally in a Hunter's arrow? Dax couldn't touch her magick then.

Her arm burned, and when she shoved back her sleeve, the silver spiral of her birthmark elongated, forming thin, pointed lines. She gasped, tracing the new mark. Had Peter's death changed her fate?

The sound of footsteps on the stairs drew her attention to the hall. She inhaled sharply, drawing up against the wall when a girl entered. Halen raised her hands to strike.

"Hey, it's just me." Nelia stood at the entrance of the kitchen, saltwater dripping from her body and pooling on the concrete. Halen's gaze rested on the silver interlocking loops of Nelia's necklace, the chain Quinn had given her as a parting gift. She wondered if Nelia would blame her for Quinn, for taking away all she had loved. Did revenge bring Nelia to her doorstep?

Halen widened her stance. "What are you doing here?"

Nelia stepped toward her.

Halen thrust her palms against the air, sending Nelia flying against the kitchen cabinets.

"I'm not here to hurt you!" She squirmed in the grip of Halen's magick.

Still, Halen kept her hands pressed against the air, lifting Nelia higher, so just the tips of her toes touched the floor. "How did you get in?"

"You left the door open."

She glanced toward the patio door. Had she forgotten to lock it when she left? No, she had been extra careful and had double-checked each lock when she got home. The alarm was definitely on now.

"How did you get in?" Halen asked again.

"Okay. I may have used a little magick, but I thought Lorn had come here first. He's an Elosian hunting sirens for Rania. I wanted to make sure you weren't hurt. I was prepared to fight for you." Her eyes pleaded for forgiveness.

Halen's magick spun with her confusion.

"Halen, listen to me. You don't have long. They're coming for you. When I heard a siren had been spotted in Rockaway, I didn't think you'd be stupid enough to come here. But then I saw the lights on... I was worried."

Her words stung. Nelia had no right to criticize her. "Where else would I go? This is my home." "Inland—as far away from the ocean as possible. Do you still have the water stone?"

Halen tightened the force holding Nelia as she spotted a diamond encrusted dagger secured at her hip. Blood flecked the tip.

Nelia followed her gaze. "I followed Lorn, but I had to take a detour because I was followed. I dragged the shifter you killed out to the ocean. You can't leave tracks behind. Not with a full-on hunt for sirens. There's an extra reward for anyone that can catch you, Natalie, or Asair. You need to get the water stone away from here and hide where they can never find you."

Nelia had fought for her behind the Mermaids' Gate. The raised scar across her neck where the mermaid struck was proof of her loyalty. Nelia had sacrificed and suffered more than most. Still, so many lies had been told. "I don't have anywhere else to go. This is all I have left."

"I know a place you can go. Do you have a car?"

"Yes, but I can't leave here."

"Go. Nothing matters but keeping you safe. I would come with you, but I'll be more of a hindrance farther inland."

"How do I know this isn't a trap?" On the road, she'd be vulnerable to an attack. But Nelia had broken into her home with simple magick. At least inland the Elosians didn't have a chance.

"Because I'm not Tari. The shifters will take care of you."

"Shifters? There's no way I'm going. A shifter just tried to kill me." She tightened her grip.

"No harm will come to you. Believe me or don't—just get the hell out before Rania surfaces."

Halen swallowed hard, fear tripping along her skin at the thought of facing Rania again. If the mermaids hadn't intervened in Elosia, Rania would have let the Krull army snap her bones one by one. She dropped her hands by her sides, allowing Nelia's feet to touch the floor.

"Thank you," Nelia said.

"You said they're hunting my sister and Asair as well—they must be alive. Do you know where they are?"

"I don't know where they are." Nelia shook her head. "But the portal to Etlis is sealed tight, so they're definitely alive. I assume they've gone into hiding. You need to do the same."

"I have to find them."

Nelia reached for the pen and paper on the counter. She scrawled a name and slid the sheet in front of Halen. "They're doing what needs to be done to keep Tarius locked away. You need to do the same. Go to this lake. The shifters there will keep you safe. No one will ever find you." A gust of wind rushed in from the living room. Nelia's gaze darted past her shoulder. "Go—now!"

This was all too much. Nelia didn't understand. She couldn't just hop in a car and drive away. She had serious baggage. And he couldn't even walk.

"Don't just stand there. Get going." Nelia shoved her toward the door while monitoring the living room.

"I can't move Dax."

"He's here? Where?" Nelia spun, searching.

"He's in there." Halen nodded toward the laundry room.

Nelia stripped away the chair barricade and flung open the door. "Oh, mercy." She slammed the door shut.

A pounding drum echoed from the patio. "I'll cover you. Use your magick." Her steel gaze met with Halen. "Be safe!" She grabbed the blade in her fist and dashed into the living room.

Trembling, Halen pocketed the address and gathered the box of vials. A part of her wanted to choke Dax for Peter's death, but like it or not, he was part of her now. She had to protect this monster.

A crash from the living room sent her already racing heart into overdrive. Blowing, she lifted Dax with her breath, so he floated. With the breeze, she directed him toward the garage while trying to drown the sounds of glass shattering in the other room.

She popped the trunk, guiding Dax's body inside, and then snatched the water stone from the floor. Her breath grew heavy as she jumped in the driver's seat. Gripping the steering wheel, she tried to steady the rising sparks, but when the garage door opened, revealing a hunched bear, her magick surged.

Fire danced across the hood and the bear released a booming growl.

Terrified she might explode in the car, she scrambled for the door when a burst of glimmering red powder rushed the flames. As the smoke cleared, Halen spotted a waif of a girl, her long copper hair flowing around her like a cape.

"Lina." Her breath rushed out all at once. She looked to the bear once more and, finding his familiar stare, she recognized Tasar.

He growled, and even though her windows remained closed, the battle cry reached inside. Had Tasar and his sister come to kill her? Whose side were they on? They both had protected her, but had things changed?

She let the window down, just a crack, when a dagger sailed through the air, poised for Lina. Halen waved, misdirecting the weapon so it stabbed the side of a wooden planter instead. Tasar nodded, his eyes gleaming with the same hope she had seen back at the church when she made spring bloom in the dead of winter. He turned, bounding toward the assailant.

Lina waved her forward. "It's safe now—go!" she yelled.

Halen drove the sedan out of the garage, stopping beside her.

Lina leaned in, clutching the window frame. "Thank you, Halen." She nodded to the blade stuck in the planter.

"What's happening?" Halen glanced toward the beach, where flames glistened along the waves.

"Rania's army surfaced. You need to leave."

"Let me fight with you."

"This isn't your battle. You must stay alive. Same as Natalie and Asair."

"Do you know where they are?" A crazed sort of panic rushed through her as she met Lina's gaze. Lina and Tasar had fought in the forest alongside them; maybe they knew where they went. "Please, if you know where they are, I need to be with them."

"You're best divided. Don't try to find them." Lina's beady, black stare cut through her.

The shifter's magick scared her. Halen knew better than to push, but she needed to know. She couldn't do this alone. "Please, tell me where they are!"

Lina shook her head. "Stay safe, Halen."

Tasar growled and Lina turned without another word, dashing toward the ocean and the wailing cries.

Halen couldn't just drive away. She had run too many times. She pounded the steering wheel, screaming. Her frustration blew out across the ocean, curling the water, forming a towering wave. She clapped her hands, and the wave crashed, washing over the surfacing Elosians. Lina glanced back, waving with gratitude, then hopped onto her brother's back. Tasar bounded along the shore as Lina cast her spell, sending glittering stars cascading from the night sky with her command. The starlight exploded in the water and the Elosians retreated.

There was no sign of Nelia, but Halen felt with Tasar and Lina by her side, she would be safe. She prayed for each of their souls as she steered the car down the alley and onto the street. As she drove away from Rockaway, loneliness washed over her. Each second spread to eternity. And she realized she may never find her way back to Natalie and Asair. They were lost to her forever.

6

THE TALL TREES faded to long stretches of sand as Halen
drove farther into Nevada. The GPS read three hours to
her destination at Pyramid Lake. At the last gas station, she
zoomed in on the map, finding nothing but desert and the
small body of water. Her magick sparked with thoughts of
shimmering liquid portals, but at least the lake wasn't as
vast as the ocean; a lake had perimeters she could monitor.

Now with her foot on the gas pedal and the distance
growing shorter between her and Nelia's shifters, she ques-
tioned more than the lake. Tari or not, Nelia had every
reason to hate her. What if this was a trap? *No one will ever
find you,* Nelia's words played through her mind. Had she
meant Natalie and Asair? Halen slammed her foot against
the brake. She needed a better plan.

She fought back a yawn. Her muscles ached and her
stomach growled for more than the bag of chips. No
wonder she couldn't think clearly. Halen needed a warm
bed but checking into a motel with Dax wasn't an option.
She yawned again, her eyelids heavy. She wouldn't be any
good to Dax if she crashed.

She pulled the car over to the side of the road, scanning the desert for signs of life, but she was alone with the
moon. "This will have to do," she said spoke out loud as
she had the whole drive just to stay sharp. Cutting the igni-

tion, she then locked the doors once, twice, and one more time just to be sure. "Twenty minutes. That should do it and then you can get on your way." Tucking her legs up to her side, she curled into the seat.

The full moon shone through the sunroof. Were Asair and Natalie staring up with dread knotting their stomachs too? "I'll find you," she whispered. "I have no idea how, but I will." Pulling her hood up, she closed her eyes, saying a prayer for her friends and asking for a way out of this catastrophic mess.

Peter's cold, dead stare plagued her mind. She winced, hugging herself tighter. As exhausted as she was, how would she ever sleep again with his death haunting her? A low hum filled the car, vibrating the seats. She opened her eyes to find the interior illuminated with a soft glow.

The source?

The water stone.

"Why are you doing that?" she asked the stone, and it burned brighter. The stone's pitch wavered with a warning that crept under her skin. Halen's sparks awoke, prickling at her fingertips, and the stone sung louder.

She peered into the darkness as she dug the keys from her pocket. Her hands shook with the sparks now rushing up her arms, and she pressed the fob by mistake. The trunk popped open with a resonating click. "Are you kidding me right now?"

The water stone squealed like an animal being led to slaughter.

"Stop!" Slapping her hands over her ears, the keys dropped to the floor.

Fighting the sparks that answered the water stone's call, she fumbled along the carpet, searching for the keys.

The car shook with a rumble.

Slowly, she peered up from the dashboard, afraid of what awaited. She bit back her screams as she met the gaze of the gnashing beast on the other side of the windshield. The coyote's fur bristled. Its black lips snarled back over canine teeth. Her magick flickered to the surface of her skin, and she clutched the seat to tame the sparks.

"Go away!" she shouted. "Please," she begged as her magick churned. She wouldn't kill again, but she didn't trust that Dax might.

The coyote growled, swaying from side to side.

She slammed her palm over the horn, but the creature didn't budge.

The car shook, this time from the above; a second canine peered in with a ravenous stare.

Her magick surged. Her gaze darted to the elixir box, to the coyote, and the now silent water stone.

The beast pawed the window, striking once, twice, three times, and the glass cracked.

"Get back!" Her cells ignited with a fiery heat when she spotted the glowing residue of magick along the shattering glass. *Shifters.*

The coyote struck the glass again, and though blood seeped through its paws, the beast hammered the fissures until the window broke away.

The desert air rushed in, charged with the static of magick. The coyote on the hood howled and the darkness bloomed with flashing eyes. One by one, the coyotes emerged, surrounding her car fortress.

Halen reached for the box of elixir, her fingers touching barely touching the box when the coyote descended from the sunroof, its teeth sinking deep into her flesh. She screamed out. Fear stirred her sparks, and she waved the coyote off. The coyote flew against the passenger window, its neck bending and its spine crushing with a crunch. As the broken canine slumped in the seat, the coyote from the hood leaped on the roof. Halen thrust both hands skyward and summoned the wind, whipping the coyote up in the air and tossing it into the pack.

The desert echoed with angry howls. Through the side mirror, she witnessed a coyote dragging Dax from the trunk. He flopped to the ground, hitting his head on the road. His forehead split with blood and Halen clutched her head where his pain cut above her brow. A coyote spread its jaws wide across Dax's neck.

"No!" She unlocked the doors, the click a warning she didn't heed. She jumped out, her feet firm on the asphalt. With a sweep of her hand, she shoved the coyote away from Dax.

She ran to his side, checking his wound. Her fingers slicked with his blood and a twisted, sickening darkness spread through her—a desire for revenge.

"*No. We can get out this.*" She fought to hold on, but Dax strangled her voice in his grip. Her sparks spun with flames. She couldn't contain the force rising inside any more than one could outswim a tidal wave.

She stood, the power of the earth at her feet, summoning the energy deep within the sand and soil, to the dusted bones of the desert dead. With her head cast skyward, the desert rose to her call with wind and flames. The sand whipped the coyotes, driving the dust down their throats, suffocating each rising howl. Flames rushed along the ground, catching in their coats, and dragging them one by one into the pyre until only the crackling of flames remained.

Halen collapsed, sobbing into her hands of death while the coyotes burned bright around her. Magick twisted in her gut, the metallic scent of blood and charred flesh choking her breath. The water stone sang, and she crawled toward the steady pulse. A wanton need consumed her, the killing both horrifying and satisfying, as if two parts of her pushed against the other, splitting her apart, with the water stone the only way to tame the quarrel.

Dax lay still, his eyes closed to the carnage surrounding them. Yet, at the seam of her soul, he savored this dark massacre. She learned one thing in this moment—if Dax couldn't free Tarius, he would unleash another demon. He would harness her powers against the world. She could see his vision as clearly as if it were her own, and this scared the hell out of her. She had to take him away—far from any beating heart. *Pyramid Lake.* Perhaps Nelia had known his intentions too. Halen would take him to the place where no one would ever find them.

But first, she needed elixir. Her skin pinched with fever, her bones aching from casting magick. As she stumbled back to the car, a young woman blurred in her vision. She emerged from the smoke, her speckled cape swaying around her. A boy stood at the woman's side, his sharp gaze boring through Halen.

The woman cupped her hands and blew, releasing a cloud of glimmering dust.

The spellbound dust spiraled, swarming Halen. She thrust her hand outward to block the dust, but it slipped between her fingers, drawing her hands down by her sides. As if bound in chains, Halen thrashed against the force. Her body lifted, floating into the air.

The boy spun, his body transforming into brown feathers, his nose elongating with a sharp hooked beak. He fluttered toward her and, with the owl boy by her side, she drifted higher, away from Dax, the elixir, and the crying water stone.

7

"ASAIR, GET IN HERE—NOW." Natalie's shouting shattered his thoughts. Asair closed his book, though he hadn't read a word, for his thoughts always wandered to Halen. His chest ached with longing; a feeling so much more over-whelming since their separation. From his dimension, when he watched over her from the orb, he yearned to know her more intimately. Now, after being a part of her, knowing her every thought, the desire to be near Halen consumed him. He understood her struggle of having so much power, and yet being tied to a Guardian that had none. Natalie found love with a Hunter, but Halen's heart was lost in the Guardian bond. The connection created a desperate loneliness that would never be filled. When Asair found her, despite the silver beneath her arm, he would find a way to set her free. He owed her at least that much.

"Asair!" Natalie's voice rose shrill.

"I'm coming." He shut the door to his bedroom, even though privacy was moot in the Hunters' fortress. He frowned as the ceiling camera rotated to follow him down the hall. The Hunters claimed the surveillance team worked for their safety and he couldn't argue the fact that he and Natalie needed protection, but he hated the idea of eyes on him twenty-four-seven, recording his every move.

He shuddered at the thought of the dozens of tapes

43

with the day-to-day-dealings of the fortress—most had been innocent, but some tapes had been too gruesome to view. Not all the Hunters murdered sirens with mercy. He couldn't fathom the idea of re-watching their kills. However, with Tage and Halen's mother, the recordings had proved useful. Asair wouldn't have agreed to come, let alone stay at the fortress if he hadn't viewed the tapes himself.

Emil and Natalie stripped their guilt away, replaying the footage in slow motion, claiming nothing could have saved Tage. Asair begged to differ. Instead of pinning the siren boy Ezra to the ceiling, Natalie should have bandaged Tage. Those few seconds may have saved the girl's life. Natalie was quick to remind him had played a part in her death, too. Had he not created the mermaids, then Tage never would have had the venom in her bloodstream. Blame was a game no one would win between sinners.

He crossed the hall and headed toward the arched doorway at the end, where the theatre speakers blared with a newscast. As he entered, Natalie's back was to him, her wavy dark hair cascading over the seat of her wheelchair, her attention fixed on the enormous panoramic screen. He stepped beside her, not caring about the news since she had already called him in three times that day for minor earthquakes in Indonesia and a flood in Venice, which had nothing to do with sirens or Halen. He figured she just liked the company. Emil, usually by her side, would lasso the moon if Natalie asked, but currently, the Hunter busied himself securing the perimeter with Vita and Jae. "What is it now?"

"I found Halen." She pressed a button on the remote.

His gaze snapped to the blurred images as she flipped through the channels. "Well, stop on one, so I can see." He held his breath as dozens of flame ravaged animal carcasses filled the screen.

"I told you it was her. The nightmares we had last night were real," Natalie said. "Dax is guiding her magick. Look at all the bodies. If we weren't already a target, now the shifters will be after us for sure."

"What has she done?" He slumped in the armchair next to Natalie. As the cameras scanned the entire massacre, Asair winced as if he had been punched in the gut. "Where is she?"

"She's closer than we thought—Nevada."

"What? She's in the same state. We have to go to her."

"Not so easy. She could be anywhere by now."

"But we can feel her. If we leave the fortress, use our bond as our guide—"

"You know we can't leave here. The other Hunters, the ones who did this to me"—she waved across her legs —"they will come for our souls. Besides, where would we start?"

"There." He pointed to the screen, where a map of the surrounding area popped up. Asair rubbed the sides of his head, pressing his temples where a new headache sprouted. He had grown accustomed to the pain of inhabiting Quinn's body. Jae had assured him in time this, too, would pass, but now the throbbing only added to his frustration.

"Putting our lives at risk is not an option."

"We have to go." His gaze slid to her wheelchair. "I can go."

"You think it's because of this." She clutched the tops of the wheels. "I may not be able to walk, but I'm just as strong as you. The arrow injured my spine, not my magick."

"I know." He sighed. "I'm sorry. You've been the bravest of us all. I just thought it might be easier if I went." He thought of the forest, the arrow piercing her back as she collapsed in Halen's arms. She would have died, her soul trapped in the gold arrow if Jae hadn't shielded her

45

with her wings and spun healing magick to stop the bleeding and the possession. Only a dragon could have saved her. Silence had consumed Natalie when Emil had brought her the wheelchair, but if it bothered her now, she didn't let it show.

Asair leaned with his back against the wall next to a bronze bust of the Hunter Otho. Seven more busts outlined the living quarters, all cast in their original bodies —a reminder of who the Hunters were before the curse. As he wrung his scarred hands, he found it hard to recall his previous appearance. Despite the headaches, he'd grown comfortable in Quinn's body; even his magick flowed through Quinn's veins as if he had been born into this vessel, and now his sparks surged. "We have to bring her here."

Natalie grabbed a blanket from the armchair and wrapped it around her shoulders. "I want to, I really do, but how? If you or I cast magick right now, we'll draw the shifters and the other Hunters right to us."

"A portal," he said, before considering the consequences. "Did you see the lake on the map—Pyramid Lake? She's close."

"Oh, no." She shook her head furiously.

"Oh, yes." He grinned. "It can't be a coincidence. Think about it. What shifters occupy the lake area? With a disturbance like this, those scavengers would surface."

"They prefer the term *collectors*. I've had my run in with the owls before. It's too risky. If we go in… If they capture us, then there's more to lose than our lives. Believe me, I want her here just as much as you, but we have to think of the collateral damage."

His mind reeled with each scenario as he paced the living room. He had witnessed many wars unfold from the orb. Asair had thought he understood the mind of a soldier better than anyone, but he hadn't factored in the feelings of the heart. He pounded the wall. "We have to do something!"

"And we will." Natalie grabbed her cell phone. "I'm calling Emil and Vita back to the fortress. We need to discuss our options."

"I could send the mermaids to the lake. They're restless in the reservoir. They would welcome the freedom, if only for a few hours."

Natalie wagged the phone at him. "No way! If Halen is there, then those fish would snap her neck. I see how they ogle over you—especially Selene. She's vindictive. You never should have summoned them here. They can't be trusted."

She was more than right. The spell bound with his blood broke when his heart stopped beating in the prison dimension, but the bond formed over a hundred years was still as strong as the day he had cast the dark magick. "They would protect Halen if I asked."

"Jealousy trumps reason. We need another way." She strummed her black painted nails against her phone.

With her this close, his magick connected with hers, the honey scented sparks begging for release. Even without the curse or a Guardian, he wondered if sirens could ever truly be free. He knelt in front of Natalie, placing his hands on her knees. His palms warmed. "You're burning up. What's wrong?"

"It's nothing." She wheeled away from his touch. "Halen may have a fever."

"You're feeling her?" He balled his hands into fists.

"Why didn't you say anything?"

"Because you're freaking out."

"Of course, I am. Doesn't any of this bother you? What if Halen's just lying in the desert, too weak to move?" He nodded toward the TV. "You know dark magick would leave her drained." He shuddered at his next thought. "What if the collectors found her—then what?"

"You're right." Natalie pulled the blanket tighter around her. "Get your fish to spin a portal then."

"Are you sure? I can go."

She let out a heavy sigh, an action that had become familiar in the Hunter's fortress—one synonymous with their rising frustration, worry, and fears. "As much as I hate saying this, you need to send the mermaids in—alone. I can't see another way."

"Even though you don't trust them?" He was stalling, but he had to run through all the possibilities. Once he asked Selene, there was no turning back.

"I trust you. And besides, if Halen doesn't have the elixir, she's screwed. Send the mermaids. At least then we'll know if she's there." She nodded toward the screen, where the cameras zoomed in on a coyote carcass. "We should have been there for her." "We didn't know." Asair bowed his head.

"I should have known! I'm her twin!" As her voice rose, the Hunters' busts rattled on the marble pillars. "If I can feel her fever, why can't I find her?"

He touched her shoulder, absorbing part of her rage until the room settled. "The curse is complicated, and then there's Dax…" He didn't want to think of him on the edge of Halen's seam.

"Do what you have to do." She glanced up, tears rimming her eyes.

"I'll speak with the mermaids after they feed," he said, though his feet wouldn't move. Asking the mermaids had been his suggestion. Why, then, did his gut twist with dread? Selene would indulge the favor, but not without a sacrifice. He feared what she would demand in return.

FLAMES BURST in the coyote's fur and its jaws split with a howl. With a wave of her hand, Halen snapped the canine's neck to silence the torturous cry. She folded, clutching her stomach as she tried to calm the trembling within, but her sparks gathered for another strike.

Dax! she shouted.

He stood wavering in the flames; his eyes alit with rage.

Stop. She begged as her magick charged. *Please.*

A coyote lunged, and she rolled into the fire, screaming until she woke with a start. She bolted upright, only to be pulled back by the thick cuffs pinning her to the ground. She wriggled, the straps burning her skin. *What the hell?* Her legs caught as well, her ankles bound by the same unforgiving material.

Where am I? Her thoughts raced. The last thing she remembered was… She let her head fall back against a pile of brush. The shifter boy—the owl gliding beside her in the smoke-filled night.

Above, a candelabra hung with crimson candles; the flames flickered, casting shadows along the dirt walls. The putrid scent of rot thickened the air. When Halen turned her head, she flinched, but her magick did not rise to greet the boy with the hungry stare.

"Who are you?" Her voice cracked.

"Danik, Danik, Danik…" His sharp yellow gaze darted to the ceiling, to the left, to the ground, and back to Halen. "My name is Danik." The boy crouched, crossing his arms over his feathery chest.

This couldn't be who bound her with these shackles—the scrawny boy could barely steady his shaking hands—but there had been another in the desert; a shifter with powerful magick.

"Where are we? Why am I bound?"

"Too much power, too much, too-too-too-too much."

Of course, she was tied—she was a murderer. Chills pinched her skin and her stomach cramped. She just wanted to curl up and rest.

"I'm cold. Can you please just loosen the bindings? I'm not feeling well." She tugged the strap attached to a gold chain and followed it to the dagger stabbed in the ground. Three more ruby encrusted daggers attached to gold chains held her in place.

"What is this place?" Her stomach rolled with her words. She swallowed, but the rising acid fought harder. She turned as the hot bile spewed from her lips.

Danik leaped up, gathering her puke in his hands. He sipped, swishing the contents of her stomach back and forth between his cheeks.

This alone churned her stomach once more, and she gagged, throwing up all over his feet.

He stepped back, still swishing her vomit in his mouth. Danik blinked, casting his gaze to the candelabra, and then spit. He swiped his mouth with the back of his hand. "Your magick is dirty. We must cleanse."

"Cleanse?" Her throat burned with the forced words. "I need elixir. Do you know what coral and bone is? There was a box in my car. If I just…" She pursed her lips to keep from throwing up again.

"No more G-g-g-uardian." He shook his head and

feathers sprouted along the part in his hairline. He clasped his hand to the new feathers, smoothing them out.

"What?" She yanked against the restraint, but it wouldn't budge. "What have you done with Dax?"

"Safe. Safe, like you, and you, and you, and you." His head jerked, bending his neck at a curiously odd angle.

Halen didn't see anyone else in the tight alcove. Perhaps he was confused. "Dax is here?"

"Safe." He rubbed his dirty hands along his pants, leaving fresh stains on the muddied suede.

Closing her eyes, she breathed through the next wave of nausea. At least they didn't leave Dax in the desert. *The water stone.* She turned toward him.

"Where's my car?"

"Gone, gone, gone."

"What does that mean? Gone where?"

He pointed to the ground. "Pria hid it. No one will find the stone."

Her mind flashed with an image of the young woman, a brown spotted feather cape draping her broad shoulders as she captured Halen with the breeze of her sparkling breath. "You hid the water stone with my car?"

"Can't touch it-t-t-t." He held up his hands; Danik's right hand was bandaged and soaked in dirt and vomit.

"I can't believe this." She rested her aching head. Coming to the desert was a disaster. She should have taken her chances at the beach house. At least there, she was free. There, she had elixir. "I'm sick. I need what was in that car. There was a box."

"The elixir is sweet." He licked his lips. "The money makes a comfy nest." He knelt and padded the cushioning beneath her.

Panic twisted her aching bones. She didn't care about the money, but not having elixir was a death sentence.

"You drank the elixir—all of it? You don't know what you've done!"

"Danik is not a fool. We needed to make sure the elixir wasn't tainted." A woman emerged from the shadows. A garland of rubies adorned her head, her yellow stare piercing. A feather cape draped her shoulders, resting over her tan hides and a small sword rested at her hip, housed in an elegant leather embossed sheath.

"The elixir isn't tainted," Halen said.

"If the elixir was harvested after your unfortunate binding"—she nodded to Halen's arm—"then it wouldn't help, anyway."

"Sister, sister." Danik leaped up, hundred-dollar bills stuck to the grime on his pants. He brushed the money away. "Her fever is worse."

"Can you check on the Guardian for me?" the woman asked. "I will look after her."

"Yes, I will taste his blood." He clapped his hands.

"That won't be necessary, Danik. Just make sure his pulse is steady." She tapped her wrist. "No need to draw blood."

He scrunched his brows as if this command disappointed him, but he nodded and departed.

"My brother had an unfortunate accident with a spell last winter. He hasn't quite been the same. But despite his speech, his magick is quite sharp."

"You're shifters." Halen knew this already, but she was hoping the woman would fill in the blanks.

"Burrowing owls." As she crouched, she swept her cape away from the vomit and side-stepped it before placing her cool hand on Halen's forehead. "We reside beneath the desert and lake. My name is Pria, and you already met my brother, Danik."

"Yes, and he drank my elixir. Please, if you have more, I need it."

"Let me loosen the bindings." She unsheathed her sword and Halen gasped. The etched steel glimmered against the candlelight. Pria touched the hilt of each ruby dagger with the tip of her sword, and the gold chains fell to dust. She secured the sword back at her side. "We had to be sure when you woke, you didn't kill us all."

"I would never..."

"But you would if you had the elixir. The drive for survival is strong in you. You could have been born Etlin."

Halen sat, rubbing her wrists where the bindings pressed into her bones.

"We'll leave those on, in case you need the chains again."

"I won't." Halen brought her knees up to her chest, and she flinched when her hair cascaded over her shoulder. She grasped a fistful of inky black locks—her once cropped hair now curled at her waist, and her hands were deep azure. "What's happened to me?"

"Death changes people—inside and out," Pria said.

Despite Halen's shocking physical appearance, this new ravenous desire twisting inside her concerned her more. Away from the wand, her body trembled with a craving to be near the water stone once more.

"Where's the stone?"

"Safe."

"You don't understand." She steadied her tone, as to not appear so desperate. "No one can find it—ever. I need it."

"We buried the stone where no one will ever find it."

"Where the hell is it?" Her voice cut with anger, and this surprised her. She wasn't attached to the stone; she had only agreed to protect it from the Tari. Otherwise, she didn't care about Galadia's wand. Still, the water stone had warned her, singing into the night before the coyotes had attacked.

"Calm down." Pria blew and the same sparkling dust, which had lifted Halen in the desert, floated around her body.

The dust swarmed Halen's mouth, drifting deep into her lungs. A calmness spread over her, soothing her frantic thoughts.

"Better?" Pria brushed the glitter off her cape.

She nodded. "But I still need the coral and bone."

"Chew this." From the lining of her cape, she pulled out a drawstring pouch. She dug inside and brought out a disk the size of a penny. She handed the purple disk to Halen.

Halen examined the tiny disk. It was much like a chewable vitamin, only the fibrous ingredients were pressed together with fine threads of shimmering gold.

"It will help with the pain."

When she touched the disk to her tongue, her mouth watered for more.

"Go on, it's not poison. I'm not an idiot. I know if you die, Etlis will open."

"Then you also know I can't stay here."

"Chew it."

Halen popped the mysterious disk in her mouth. As she chewed, the disk dissolved into a creamy sweet center.

"Good." Pria swept her braid off her shoulder. "I can't give you elixir, but Danik's potions will make the withdrawal easier."

"What?" She swallowed the rest whole. "I need to find the others. My sister and Asair, do you know where they are?"

"They aren't important." She shook her head. "Your focus is to be free of your Guardian. Otherwise, your magick is useless. Look at your arm. You've killed many." Her voice held no tone of accusation.

Halen studied her new birthmark; the patterns were no

longer soft curlicues and starbursts. Now, dozens of sharp silver lines slashed her arm, same as the one that formed when Peter died. Her breath rushed out all at once. "This is their lives—the shifters I killed?"

She nodded. "Death also never lets you forget."

"This is not who I am." She choked back the rising tears. "This not who I want to be."

"You were born a warrior. Sometimes, to win battles, lives must be sacrificed. Don't be ashamed."

"You don't understand. Dax harnessed my magick. He made all of this happen."

"Then you have much to learn." She guffawed.

"I need to be with my sister and Asair. They can help me."

Pria dropped a handful of purple disks in Halen's lap. "They will help with the pain."

"You can't keep me here."

"If you want to find your way out, go ahead. But we can't help you if you're lost. The tunnels stretch for miles."

"Now is not the time to wean me off Dax. I don't even think it's possible." She held up her arm. "We're bound."

"We'll see."

"Rania is coming for me. I need my magick."

"We are aware of the situation. For now, we'll protect you and your Guardian. That was the deal."

"Deal? What deal?" Her pulse raced. Who would speak on her behalf? Whoever it was sure as hell didn't like her. Halen would never send a friend here.

"The deal we made with the Elosian girl from the lake." From her pocket, Pria withdrew a silver necklace with two interlocking loops; the parting gift from Quinn.

When Asair gave the necklace to Nelia, Halen had thought it odd, especially when Asair told Nelia she would know what to do with it. Is this what Quinn had in mind? They couldn't have known it would all come to this. Still,

Nelia hadn't hesitated when she had written the destination on the scrap paper.

"You're protecting me for a necklace? There has to be more. What are you getting out of this?"

Pria smiled the same twisted grin as her brother's. "Your magick."

"What do you mean? My magick isn't transferrable." She clasped her hands against her racing heart.

"But each part of you is powerful, every single cell. Every,"—she wrapped her finger around a lock of Halen's hair—"part of your body."

Halen's eyes widened.

"Even those beautiful green eyes will be mine once we separate you from your Guardian."

"Etlis will open." Halen shrunk back from Pria.

"I don't need your soul. I only want parts of you. It's a shame your heart must beat. So much power in one organ." She turned with a sweep of her cape. "Take your medicine. You're going to need it." She disappeared down the tunnel.

Halen's fear stirred. Could she really cut her to bits and use her magic? Had this been part of Nelia's revenge? Her breath quickened. No way was she staying to find out. She would take her chances in the tunnels.

9

RESERVATION HUNG like a noose around Asair's neck as he made his way to the reservoir. The mermaids were his responsibility—his abomination.

Over the decades, observing the sisters from his dimension, remorse for his actions tore at his conscience. With the spell now broken, the bond hinged on Selene's black heart, and as much as he hated the bond, he needed the mermaids. They were his eyes on the outside. If they went to Pyramid Lake and Halen was near, they would sense her presence, and if he asked, they would bring her back to him. At least, he hoped to the heavens they would.

He caught his reflection in the tinted windows as he passed the control center. Gone was the ghostlike boy with long, flowing, snow-white hair and stark complexion. Now a rugged young man with shaved black hair stared back, his skin a warm umber tone, not like Quinn's mother Rania, but like his human father.

He rubbed his hand across the stubble on his chin and over the raised scar trailing his neck. He couldn't imagine Rania standing by while the Elosians inflicted these wounds on her son. When their souls had merged, Asair had understood Quinn's pain, had relived each lashing and tortured cry as if he too had suffered an Elosian trial. And though the siren no longer remained present, Asair would ensure his fight was never forgotten. He admired the boy who had sacrificed his life for the realms; he wouldn't let him down.

A damp fog enveloped him when he pushed open the heavy steel door. The water churned with choppy waves as silver tails slipped between the crests, sending a shiver down his spine. Though the tank measured forty feet deep, restraining the mermaids this way was like keeping a whale in an aquarium. They couldn't thrive here.

He approached the edge with caution, never quite knowing the mood of the girls. Selene popped up first, no doubt lurking near the surface, awaiting his arrival. She swam to the edge, propping her silver scaled elbows on the concrete. Her wispy dark hair wrapped around her shoulders like a cape of snakes. Still, beneath the scales, he recalled the beautiful Elosian, her skin glistening with dew, her eyes wide with life and devotion; her petal pink lips, which once sipped his blood, were now stained black from the curse he had once held over her.

"Where have you been?" She slapped her tail against the water.

Her two sisters, Kye and Diya, surfaced, responding to her request. Out of twelve, only three remained; two turned to stone at Halen's hand, which only made his request that much more difficult to ask.

"I have some good news." His skin flecked with warning sparks as he crouched to be level with Selene. She liked him close, and even though the proximity turned his stomach, he needed to appease her.

Her incisor teeth punctured her bottom lip as her smile broadened. She licked away the black blood. "You look hopeful today." Her gleaming gaze skimmed his, searching for a way into his thoughts. "Are we going somewhere?"

He glanced away, knowing already she'd seen in too far. "We may have found her." His tone remained flat. He didn't even say *her* name to not appear eager. He feared Selene's tantrum if she read his confused emotions.

"You found the siren?" The smile slipped from her mouth.

"It took you long enough." Kye joined her sister by the ledge while Diya circled, her curious gaze trained on him.

Asair's pulse raced as they read him, each mermaid confirming every heartbeat still belonged to them. "We believe she's with the owls beneath Pyramid Lake. I need —" He paused. "*We* need you to go and see. If she's there, bring her back with the Guardian."

"Oh, I do like the Guardian." Kye pushed away from the ledge, floating back, and fanning her fins across the surface. "His blood is so sweet." The tips of her tail curled as she laughed.

Diya licked her lips. "I am a little hungry for something other than the dry desert birds your dragon brings us. Their organs reek of land. And the aftertaste…"

"You can't harm him," Asair warned, cutting her off. "We need his marrow." He rubbed his forehead where the previous headache collided with a new one. Asking them to bring Halen back safely was a horrible idea. Cooped up with little to feed on, they needed to hunt. He feared where this venture would lead.

"You can't drain his blood, Kye." Selene rolled her eyes. "The blue moon siren is weak without him. She's not like us."

"No, she's nothing like you," Asair spoke through gritted teeth, though he kept his tone warm.

Selene strummed the concrete ledge, her black nails razor-sharp, able to slice through his flesh with one swipe. Yet, he was sure she wouldn't harm him. At least, he hoped her love for him would protect him. She wouldn't stay at the fortress otherwise. The shifters may be masters of portals, but Selene and her sisters were masters at blocking them. Already, they had blocked a dozen attempts at entering. "If she is with the owls, then they won't give her up without a fight."

"Or a trade," Kye said.

"What do *we* get in return?" Selene asked.

He swallowed hard, glancing toward the door. He shouldn't have come. "I don't have much to give."

Kye giggled as black smoke rose from the water.

He stood, stepping away at once. "Not today." Of all days, he couldn't allow them to see into his mind. Not when every thought centered on Halen.

Selene's tail rolled above her like a scorpion, and he steadied his breath. He couldn't help but feel she had already peeked inside his brain. "We will fetch her *if* you promise to leave with us when we return."

He crossed his arms, hiding his clenched fists against his rib cage. "You know I can't leave the fortress."

"Because you have feelings for the siren?" Selene met his gaze.

"No." He glanced away, hoping she didn't read the lie in his eyes. He cared for Halen. It was true. But not in the way Selene believed. Still, Selene would interpret his concern and guilt as more. "We need her alive. Even though the curse breaks, you live because of the magick I cast." He crouched once more, leaning close to the water. He lowered his voice, using Quinn's seductive alto tones. "If the portal opened, we would never see each other again."

Playing with Selene's emotions was cruel, but the soul of the girl who sipped his blood so many years ago no longer remained. Black magick tainted the demon's heart now. "What you're reading is Jae's spell. I'm connected to Natalie *and* Halen. There's nothing I can do about it."

Selene rose out of the water, stopping inches from his nose. Though her breath, laced with a putrid sulfur scent, roiled his gut, he didn't budge. Revealing his repulsion now would only endanger Halen.

She locked with his gaze. Eye to eye, she attempted to claw her way into his thoughts. His head pulsed as his magick pushed back, fighting the force of Selene as she ripped away at each stitch of his protection spell. Shackled by the force of her powers, he fought for a firm footing in their mental game of tug-of-war.

But he slipped. For just one second. His mind flooded with a vast poppy field, tall grass swaying in the ocean breeze. On the bluff, a girl with flowing chestnut hair called out his name. As Halen stood before him, his magick ignited.

Selene broke the bond, slipping from the ledge, and dived beneath the water, taking the sweet vision with her.

Panic rushed through his veins, pumping his heart with dread. "Wait!" He reached, and her fins slid past his fingers.

Diya laughed. "You never were good at blocking your emotions, Asair." She dived, following her sister.

His thoughts filled with dread as he scanned the water, debating whether he, too, should dive in after Selene.

Kye splashed the water with her tail. "Don't worry. We won't harm the siren. We could have killed her already. We've always known where she was." A mischievous grin played on her lips.

"You what? You knew, and you didn't tell me?" He dropped his fists by his sides.

"Does it matter if you don't care about her?" Kye winked.

"It matters because we need to protect her. Or do you want to die too?"

"Halen's not as innocent as you think. She's a killer. She would be beautiful with a tail." She bobbed on her back, fanning her silver fins in his face. "We could teach her things. Her magick is so—"

"Kye!"

"Relax." She cackled with delight.

The sound grated on his nerves.

"I'm just not into you the way my sister is." She dipped her fins back underwater. "I'm more interested in the boy —the Guardian." She swam to the ledge, popping up inches from him. "Promise Dax to me and no harm will come to Halen."

"You can't have him!" He didn't back away. As much as he hated Dax, he couldn't let anything happen to Halen's Guardian. "He's not a toy."

"And what did you think of us when we drank your blood?" She drifted back, spreading the water with her webbed fingers. "My sister still loves you. I will do whatever it takes to make her happy." "Kye," his voice held warning.

"The boy is mine." She dived beneath the water without waiting for his reply.

He slammed his fist against the concrete, his magick cracking fine fissures along the floor. Regret knotted his stomach, wishing he could take back his request.

10

WAITING for Pria to chop her into pieces was not on Halen's agenda. She had had enough of everyone thinking they could do what they wanted with her magick. Especially Dax. But if Pria found a way to him, could the shifter pull her strings and unleash the power of the darkness within? Already, a craving tempted Halen to that side of her seam more than she cared to admit. She was ashamed of the wanderlust the dark magick left in her heart. She couldn't allow this part of herself to bloom into a twisted garden for Pria to tend.

Despite each movement stabbing her inside and out, she inched toward the wall. With her back pressed against the rock, she slid up to her feet. The flickering candlelight blurred her vision, making the chamber whirl. She popped another one of Pria's disks, chewing quickly while she closed her eyes to keep from toppling back to the ground. As the spins subsided, she blinked away the dizzy feeling, and the chamber steadied in her vision. Ahead, a dark tunnel awaited. She only had to gather enough strength to get there.

"You can do this." She took a careful step forward. Her knees buckled, and she grasped the wall to keep her balance.

A cry cut the air, raising the hairs at the back of her neck.

Was someone else having their magick harvested? She shuddered, her panic stirring. "Get it together, girl." She took another step. Whether it was the pellet kicking in or the sheer fear of Pria coming back and cutting her to bits, her steps steadied.

As she entered the tunnel, darkness enveloped her. She shivered, though heat pressed around her. The giggle of babbling babies echoed from above and she pressed against the rock, making herself as small as possible. The laughter reverberated off the walls, bouncing around her. She clasped her hand over her mouth to stifle her screams. The babies broke out with wails as if torn away from their mothers.

Blinded by the darkness, she wondered if actual babies watched her from above or if this was some sick alarm alerting her escape. Shuffling against the wall, she quickened her pace. Halen followed the curves of the tunnel, not knowing which way was out. She thought of the shifter's warning and feared being lost forever. She needed Dax to show her the way.

Dax was connected to her and the last thing he wanted was to die. He had made that very clear in the desert. He would kill to live. And right now, the only way to survive was for her to find him and get the hell out of this owl trap.

She called to him from deep within, summoning Dax to guide her to him now. Forcing out the chilling laughter, she focused her thoughts on Pria's intentions and to the emanate danger they both faced if they didn't escape. Even though Dax craved her magick as his own, he was born to protect her. If he wanted any part of her power, if he truly believed in Tarius, then he wouldn't let Pria possess her magick. No matter who Dax served, he needed to help, or they would both lose everything.

With her thoughts centered on Dax, she headed farther down the tunnel. *Can you hear me?* He didn't answer. *We'll die if you don't help. No shot at Tarius then...* She tried baiting him, but the farther she walked, the louder the babies wailed and she worried Pria would find her first.

Ahead, she caught the glimmer of candlelight. Her breath hitched. Could this be where they were keeping Dax? She inched closer. The wailing babies hushed and this, too, frightened her, for she understood all too well the calm before a storm. She shook her hands, searching for her sparks, but they didn't rise. She wondered, too—if she cast her magick, would it save her, or would she crumble? Without elixir, she feared the latter. Either way, she would fight.

She peeked around the corner and her chest caved, her breath stolen at the sight before her. Her gaze darted between each dark swirl, each triangle and dot of the Elosian birthmarks, and to the desperate gazes of the caged sirens. She stepped into the light.

"Who are you?" a girl asked. She clutched the bars, her knuckles scabbed, her pinky fingers severed.

A wail echoed from within the walls, and the siren pursed her lips.

Another siren, a boy about Halen's age, came forward, gently taking the girl's hands from the bars and pulling her away. He had the same copper-flecked hair as the girl, his shoulders broad, his arm amputated. "You should leave," he said to Halen.

She studied the other sirens, each missing some part of their body—a limb, a finger, an ear. A child pushed his way to the bars, and where a left eye should be, a yellow fish tail poked out. When he turned his head, the tail flopped as if waving.

"Did Pria do this to you?" Halen asked, her anger spinning inside her and the dirt at her feet swirling. She bit back the burning pain of the sparks riding along her veins, but she couldn't contain her rage. Who would hurt a child?

"It's her." The boy with the fish tail eye spoke. "Even without my oracle eye, anyone can see it's the blue moon siren."

"Shh. Lower your voice. Pria will hear," the boy with the copper hair said.

"No one can hear anything over those damn water babies crying." A stout man with a full white beard studied Halen as if she were the one in the cage. "What's wrong with her?"

"She needs medicine," the boy with the copper hair said.

"Like this?" The young boy with the fish tail eye asked, holding up an elixir vial.

Saliva filled Halen's mouth. "Where did you get that?" She crawled toward them.

"Danik made me drink it. It's disgusting." The boy shrugged.

"Toss it to me, please." She held out her hands.

The boy rolled the bottle along the ground. She grasped it in her fist and tilted the bottle back. Only a drop hit her tongue. Not near enough to replenish her powers. "Is there more?"

"Danik has the rest," the boy with the copper hair said.

"Who are you?" Halen asked.

"Can you get us out of here?" The girl shook the bars.

"Lacelle, no. She needs to get out of here." The boy shook his head.

"I'm not leaving you here." Halen fumbled to her feet, wiping the dirt along her jeans.

The girl smiled, revealing bare gums. When she met

Halen's gaze, she covered her mouth with her hand and turned away.

"What did they do to you?" She stepped to the cage and faced the boy. She noticed his eyes were Elosian green with flecks of gold, which sparkled against the candlelight. He had a tortured stare, eyes that had seen too much for his age—siren eyes.

"I'm Lacelle, and this is my brother, Luke," the girl said, breaking the silence between them.

Halen glanced away at once and nodded to the girl. "My name is Halen."

"I'm Orca," said the young boy with the fish eye. "And this is Boris, our uncle."

The bearded man nodded.

"Harry and Faisal don't speak." Lacelle motioned to two sirens at the back of the cage. "Pria cut out their tongues."

They bowed their heads.

She couldn't believe her eyes. "I'm getting you out of here." She grappled with the two metal locks binding the cage. "Where do they keep the keys?"

"Danik has the keys," Luke said, "and our spells are useless in here."

"You can cast magick?" This shouldn't surprise her. But then again, Ezra had been a siren who hadn't known the first thing about spells.

"We each have our strengths. Pria thought maybe it was part of us." The girl traced a triangle in the dirt with her toe. "Maybe she's right. Since she took my teeth, I can't remember my spells properly."

Luke took the girl's hand in his. "It's okay, we'll find another way."

"How did you get here?" Halen tugged the lock.

Lacelle slipped her hand from Luke's and dipped her fingers in the pockets of her dress. "We fled to the desert when the fire rings hit San Francisco." Her voice cracked with tears.

Luke continued. "The Hunters killed our grandfather. We just wanted to get away, so we came to our uncle in the desert. He, too, was under attack with Faisal and Harry. Pria offered us all a place to hide. We didn't know the cost."

"This is all my fault." Her sparks stirred with anger once more. "We'll find a way out." Halen closed her eyes. She called deep inside to her waning magick. The sparks ripped at her cells, tugging her worn muscles, but she dragged the force to her flesh.

The locks rattled.

Her hand shook as she gathered the sparks. Halen harnessed the dirt at her feet, channeling the strength of the earth to her command, and with her next breath, black smoke passed her lips. She blew, and the smoke curled inside the locks, finding the fit, and they popped open. She grasped the bars to keep from falling.

Luke reached through, releasing the locks, and the door swung open.

"That was epic." Orca gaped up at his brother. "You have to admit, Luke, she's spectacular."

"Thanks for your vote of confidence, but my magick is not what it should be." She stumbled, and Luke caught her under his arm.

He wrapped his hand around her waist, pulling her to her feet. "Do you mind?"

"Thank you." Halen glanced up at him and smiled.

"I don't think I can walk on my own. My legs feel like jelly."

The babies screeched with an alarming cry as if knowing what she had done.

"Let's get out of here." Orca took Lacelle's hand. "Do you remember the way?"

Lacelle nodded. "Of course. I'm still good with directions."

"You go," Halen said. "I have to find my Guardian." Her knees buckled and Luke pulled her in close.

"We're going with you," he said.

Boris shot his nephew a warning glance.

"She's a siren like us. We leave together," Luke said.

Faisal and Harry nodded in agreement.

Halen looked at the sirens before her. She understood now why Tage had pushed Ezra and her away—her bullet-proof attitude hadn't been to protect herself, but to distance herself from others to save their lives. "No. Get out while you can."

"Not an option. Sirens stick together." Luke grinned. "We're the only ones we can trust."

"Look, this is dangerous." She met his determined stare. "I don't know what's ahead. Just leave before Pria comes."

"If Pria cuts you up, none of us will be okay." Orca tapped the side of his head. "I've seen that already." He faced Boris. "You're going to die whether or not you help her. So at least do the right thing."

"Humph. Thanks, kid." Boris rubbed the top of Orca's head. "But I'm not dying anytime soon. I will help, though. We can't just leave her here after she helped us."

"Good." Luke's face spread with a wide grin. "So where are they keeping your Guardian?"

She didn't like this one bit, but she didn't have the energy to argue. She barely had the strength to stand. "We need to go that way." Halen pointed. "That's where Dax is. At least that's where I'm feeling his energy." She sighed. If she took one wrong turn…

"Faisal and Harry, walk ahead," Luke said. "Lacelle and Orca, you go behind us, and Uncle Boris, you pick up the rear."

69

"Always the ass." He rolled his eyes.

"Hee-haw." Orca let out a trill donkey cry.

"Stop it now,"—Lacelle tugged his hand—"or the water babies will hear you."

Faisal and Harry headed into the tunnel, and they followed.

The cries grew louder, sending chills along Halen's already fevered skin. "Are those the water babies? What are they?"

"Demons from the lake," Lacelle said at her back.

"We're all cursed."

"Cursed?" Halen asked.

"My sister believes in the legends of Pyramid Lake. If you hear the water babies cry, then you'll be cursed with bad luck… If you look one in the eyes, you'll die. But it's just a spooky tale."

"The water babies are real," Lacelle said.

"I've never seen one," Orca said. "And I don't want to."

"I don't either," Halen said.

"Don't tell me you believe in fairy tales," Luke laughed.

"Fairy tales don't scream. And after everything I've seen, I'm not taking my chances."

"How did you get here?" Boris's voice boomed in the tunnel.

"Shh," Lacelle warned.

"How did they find you?" He lowered his voice.

She wished now she'd just walked in silence. If they knew the truth, they'd run. "They captured me in the desert."

"Even with all your magick?" Surprise flecked Luke's voice.

"She was drained." Orca piped up. "I've seen it all." Halen flinched. Had the boy witnessed the massacre?

"What's wrong?" Luke nudged her forward.

"Nothing. I'm just a little tired," she said.

"I wish I had all that power," Lacelle said. "I would—"

"Stop." Halen braced her hand on the wall. "He's through here."

"I don't see anything." Boris huffed.

"No one can see anything," Luke said.

"She's right." Orca stepped beside her. Halen felt his soft hair at her elbow.

The boy took her hand in his. "Step through."

She didn't even have a second to hesitate as he pulled her to the other side.

She blinked, adjusting to the light. Her heartbeat rushed with her frantic breath when she looked across the cave. A pool of water gurgled with onyx water. Dax floated in the center on a bed of water lilies, and the stems bound his wrists and ankles. A little hand reached up and pinched his skin. Halen gasped, and the creature turned. Its gleaming red eyes met with her, and it cried out, wailing.

"Don't look." Lacelle grabbed her sleeve.

But Halen couldn't tear her gaze away. Beyond the demon infant, a boy stood, his eye twitching when his stare landed with her. She slipped from Luke's grip, the shock sending her to the ground. "Catch?"

CATCH RETRACTED a needle from Dax's hip. His eyes blinked, twitching in over time. "Halen, what are you doing here?"

"You're working with them?" Her mind raced. The last time she had seen him, he had been with Dax in Elosia. She thought Catch had died, but really, she hadn't known what had happened to him. She just never expected to find him below the desert, with her Guardian, and working for the enemy.

"I don't have a choice." When he stepped toward her, his leg caught in the gold chain fastened to the wall. A little hand reached up and clawed his leg, drawing blood.

"Water babies," Lacelle whispered at her back.

"We're all going to die."

"Stop that." Catch kicked the hand, unleashing the cry of the babies. "Silence," he shouted, "or you won't have any more blood!"

The wailing stopped at once.

"I thought you were safe." Catch turned his attention back to Halen. "I had no idea you were here. I was trying to figure out how to get the silver out of Dax. So, you could be free. How did this even happen?"

"I screwed up," Halen said. "When I took the water stone, the bracelets melded under our skin."

"Water stone magick." Catch nodded. "That makes sense."

"What the hell is all this?" Luke walked toward the black water with Halen by his side.

Another hand reached up and pinched Dax's skin.

"What are they doing?" Halen cringed as a hand pinched his calf.

"It's good for his circulation," Catch explained. "They aren't hurting him."

"I wouldn't trust them," Lacelle said.

Halen didn't know what to think. She'd been betrayed before, and the greatest trust broken had been by the boy floating on the bed of flowers in front of them. "How did you get here?"

"After Pepper died,"—his voice cracked—"I had to leave Elosia. I didn't have a reason to stay, anyway. Pepper was my best friend." He bowed his head.

"I'm so sorry," Halen said. "I tried to help her." She really had, but Asair blocked her magick and Dax just let Pepper go.

"I'm sure you did your best." He wrung his hands.

"Why did you come here of all places?" she asked.

"Pyramid Lake has always been a portal for Elosians who enjoy human comforts."

Halen wasn't buying it. The coincidence was too convenient. Plus, he was good friends with Nelia; had they planned this together? "Did Nelia send you here?"

"What—no?" His eye stopped blinking. "Why would you think that? Is she here too?"

"No, but she sent me to the lake." She crossed her arms.

"I don't know why she would." Catch ran his hand over his bald head. "Pyramid Lake used to be part of the inland sea. It's a well-known portal—I swear."

"He's telling the truth," Luke said. "It's one reason so

many sirens are in Nevada, or why they used to be until the Hunters built their fortress here. They liked the easy hunting grounds."

"That's sick," Halen said.

"My friend Desmond lives nearby. I came to be with him," Catch said.

His explanation still didn't add up in Halen's mind. "But how? You can't be on land long."

"We've always made it work." His eye blinked.

"That is until Danik found us. I had a choice—Desmond's life or mine. I couldn't lose anyone else. I've been here, working, sharing my knowledge of potions and magick. What little I know. I couldn't believe it when they brought Dax in. You should leave—all of you."

"He's right," Boris chimed in from behind.

"I can't leave without Dax." She turned to Luke. She wasn't sure about Catch's story. It was plausible he had a friend in the desert, but she also remembered the Elosians had banned him from coming to Earth. This person would have to be pretty special for Catch to risk his life, and yet he had never mentioned him before.

"How do we get him out of there?" Luke edged back when another little hand reached up and pinched Dax.

Catch touched a lily bloom; the flower growled and snapped shut. "You can't take him without a trade. The water babies can tame the flowers, but they will want something in return." His twitchy gaze darted to Halen. "I'm sure they would settle for some of your blood."

"Don't do it," Lacelle warned.

"I hear voices." Boris's voice came out as a growl. "I think someone's coming."

Faisal and Harry widened their stances, blocking the way from where they had entered.

If this was a trap, she would need magick to save them. She needed coral and bone. "Do you have elixir?"

"I can make some." Catch grabbed another needle. "I don't have any coral though, so it might burn like hell going down."

Pria mentioned something about tainted elixir; she wasn't sure his marrow was a good idea. "Dax took my magick to some pretty dark places. I need the elixir from my car."

"Danik has it. Though, I don't know how much is left."

"Whatever you're going to do, do it now." Boris joined Faisal and Harry at the entrance. "Whoever it was turned the other way, but it doesn't mean another owl won't show up any minute."

"I'll make the trade with the water babies." Halen thrust out her arm.

"No." Lacelle yanked her back from the water.

"I've been through worse. A little blood for my Guardian is a fair trade." She pushed up her sleeve. "Also, extract the marrow." She turned to Catch. "I can't afford to be any weaker, and we need to get you out of here too." She pointed to the chain. "I can't break it without magick."

"Just take Dax." Catch wriggled the chain. "I won't survive the desert. Desmond's probably far away by now. At least I hope so."

"We have an Elosian mother," Luke said. "We'll take you to safety."

Halen glanced up at Luke. "Thank you."

"I guess I should start believing in fairy tales." He smiled.

"You've got to believe in something."

"I believe in your powers. Do what you need to do."

She wished she'd met this rugged boy before. But it's not like he'd have been wandering down her school halls. She wondered what his life had been like growing up; had he always been so brave, so sure? She hadn't always known what to do, except right now, at this moment. Dax might drag her to the dark side, but she wouldn't let them die in this wretched place.

"Extract some marrow." Halen nodded to Catch.

"Are you sure?" Orca asked.

"I need my magick," Halen said. "I'm too weak to fight without it."

"We can fight. We know spells." Lacelle said.

"You haven't been able to get out so far. If you're right and they took your powers, you won't survive."

"She's right," Catch said. "I don't like the idea of giving her Dax's marrow, either. Especially when I don't have the coral to balance it, but this may be your only way out of here. We need to hurry."

Orca shook his head, and the fish tail flopped side to side. "I see death."

"What do you want to do?" Luke looked to the others. "We make this decision together."

"Do it now." Boris clenched his fists. "We've already wasted too much time."

Lacelle and the boys nodded.

Luke turned back to Halen. "If you turn on us, I will have to strike back."

"I understand," Halen said. "Catch, extract the marrow." When she dipped her hand in the water, her finger pricked. "Ouch." She withdrew, clasping her hand to her chest.

A chubby, round face appeared. The water baby's eyes glowed, but she dared not look it straight on, fearful of Lacelle's warning. "You had a taste. If you want more, you need to let my Guardian go." The baby giggled.

"Do we have a deal?"

Dozens of little heads popped up from the water. Their mouths pulled back over pointed fangs, and a hiss filled the air.

"Holy hell." She gasped, backing away.

Luke grasped Halen's shoulder. "We'll find another way."

"Catch?" Halen looked to her friend extracting the needle.

"I've got enough," he said.

She thrust her hand out to grab the syringe, but a high-pitched screech sent Catch's already shaky hand into spasms, and he dropped the needle in the water, the water babies diving after it.

Another high-pitched screech cut through the air. Faisal and Harry flattened their backs against the wall as the rocks from which they had passed through faded.

Danik appeared at the opening. His head bobbed from side to side as he studied the scene before him.

"What, what, what-t-t-t is this?"

"They're escaping, you fool." Pria pushed past him.

Boris slipped in behind her. He pulled Pria against his chest, brandishing a blade at her throat. Magick cracked in the air as Pria thrust the hulk of man back with a dismissive wave. He hit the ground, crying out in pain.

Lacelle lunged, but the siren boy, Faisal, dragged her back.

Harry clocked Pria with a blow to her head.

"St-t-t-op!" Danik grabbed a bottle from his waist. He ripped the top off with his teeth and blew, sending a rich indigo powder into the air.

"Take cover!" Luke shouted. "Don't breathe it in."

Harry let go, covering his mouth with the crook of his elbow, while Lacelle buried her face against Faisal's chest.

Orca darted for Danik, shoving him to the ground. Danik squirmed beneath the boy, screaming. "Pria hee-e..." But his sister was on the other side of the blue cloud.

Orca pinned his arms with his knees. "You have something of mine." He dug his fingers deep inside Danik's eye socket, ripped out his eye, and shoved it in his pocket.

"Give it back!" Danik shouted.

Grasping the fish tail in both hands, Orca tugged. His head jerked as the tail grew longer and longer until forming the sleek body of a serpent. The shimmering scaled creature writhed in the boy's hands, but when it spotted the empty eye socket, the serpent slipped free from his grip and dived.

"No, no, no, nooo!" Danik fought the slithering creature burrowing into his skull.

Harry scooped Orca from the ground while the beating sound of wings boomed in the chamber.

"We need to leave now," Lacelle shouted. She crouched by Halen, pointing. "There's one behind your friend. Give the baby your blood and let's get out of here before the others come."

"Hurry." Catch waved her forward.

"You want my blood?" She wriggled her finger in the murky pond, drawing the water baby's attention.

The baby nodded.

She offered her arm, extending it over the water.

Her eyes widened when its gums sprouted with fangs. "Come on," Halen beckoned the baby over, despite her fear.

The infant clasped her arm, its grip like ice, and sunk its teeth into her flesh. She cried out as the baby suckled her wrist. Halen's energy waned, and the pond spun in her vision.

"Enough!" Catch grabbed the baby by its ankle, dragging it away. "Free the Guardian."

The water baby gnawed at the lily bindings, and Dax floated free.

"Free him too." Halen pointed to Catch.

The baby released a loud belch, and Catch's chains fell to dust. The infant dived back under as owls streamed in, beating the indigo dust with their wings. "Halen." Catch grabbed two vials from his workstation. "You need to dive in." He smashed the vials together, releasing a putrid odor.

Halen slapped her hand over her mouth and nose, wondering what in the world he had done when the owls froze midair.

"You have thirty seconds, tops." Catch gathered potion bottles up in his arms. "Go now."

"I'm not going in there." Lacelle searched for another way out, but the owls blocked the tunnel exit.

"It's the only way," Catch said.

Luke scooped up his sister with one arm and tossed her in. Lacelle screamed, batting the water.

Harry dived in with Orca, who now had a shiny gold eye in his socket. "It is this way." Orca swam to Lacelle. "I can see the way out clearly. Follow me." He disappeared beneath the dark water.

"Orca!" Lacelle dived.

Faisal, his skin scratched from shoulder to foot, jumped into the pond and dived with Harry.

"Let's go." Halen set one foot on the ledge.

"Uncle Boris!" Luke called out while searching between the blue dust and feathers. His uncle lay across the cavern, his flesh picked away from the bones.

"Go!" Boris shouted.

"Go with the others." Luke's voice cut with desperation as he turned to Halen. "I can't leave him."

Halen should leave. Bound to the curse sealing Tarius, her life mattered the most. At least that was what Jae or Asair would argue. But she had left Asair in the forest to fend for himself, and she wished every second she had stayed to fight. Already, she admired Luke's allegiance to the others. Perhaps, if sirens fought together, there would be less to fear. "I'm not going anywhere. We'll get your uncle together." She stepped down from the ledge and the owls screeched back to life, batting the air with dizzied flight.

Luke's face turned with a frown as he shielded his head. "No. Take your Guardian and get the hell out of here. I know what your life means to us—to Etlis."

"I can't leave you here." Halen ducked, dodging an owl. "I won't."

His eyes widened with a fear Halen recognized all too well. "Get back." He dragged her away from the pond, pulling her against his chest.

Silver fins flashed in the black water, slipping in and out of the spinning current. Halen's sparks ripped along her skin. The water gurgled as black smoke rose in the air, and the owls screeched louder.

"What is that thing?" Luke hugged her tighter.

Halen turned away as a fin slapped the water, sending a wave across the cavern. "Hell."

12

DRAINED from the suckling water baby and without elixir, Halen's magick fizzled with each breath. "Find your uncle." She pushed against Luke's chest.

"We stick together." Luke widened his stance.

She feared his whole ride-or-die attitude would end up in the latter. "You can't fight the mermaids. You need to run."

Talons curled up from the water and the mermaid snagged Dax, dragging him into the pond.

"No!" Halen stumbled and she fell with her chin inches above the murky water. A face marred with black veins rose to greet her. Two mermaids surfaced behind; the deadly trio focused on her.

An owl swooped overhead, drawing the attention of one mermaid. With a snap of her fingers, the water rose, coating the ceiling, dripping down the walls, and surrounding them in a bubble. The owls cried out as their feathers soaked, dragging them to the ground. With another click of the mermaid's fingers, the water cascaded, flooding the cavern.

Two mermaids rushed from the pond and slithered through the cavern, plucking the thrashing owls, and crushing them one by one.

Boris lay on the other side, clutching his chest. Faisal

and Harry each got caught in tangles of wings and magick while they battled to get to the man's side. Luke darted in and out of the bird's chaos, running for his uncle.

"Shift!" Pria commanded. She dropped her cape and rolled her shoulders back as the dark mermaid sisters advanced.

The owls beat the water, transforming into limbs and flesh. An army of stout, muscled men and women crawled to their knees, but the mermaids were an unforgiving storm no one would survive.

A girl, not much older than Halen, widened her stance. Her hands shook and she tightened her fists. The mermaid let out a haunting howl, but the girl remained steady.

The mermaid lunged. The shifter girl struck out, but the mermaid ripped her arm off with a swift bite and the girl collapsed, screaming as her blood seeped into the water.

Halen's breath rushed in and out as memories of the Krull army, mermaids ripped to pieces, flashed in her mind.

A shifter man cried out as black talons hooked his jaw, tearing his mandible from his face. His tortured gaze found Halen before the mermaid tossed him aside.

A mermaid rushed the shifters, snapping a woman's neck; the other shifters didn't even turn as they bolted for the tunnel. One by one, the sea witches plucked their victims from the ground like weeds.

Guided by the threat of survival, what little magick lingered in her veins now forced its way to Halen's finger-tips. She fought for breath as the sparks utilized her strength, ripping and tearing at her cells, sucking the marrow from her bones—if life existed inside her worn body, her magick sought it now.

The mermaid tossed the girl's arm and scanned the

cavern for her next victim. Her gaze targeted the young man cradling his uncle.

"Luke, watch out!" Halen waved, commanding the water, collecting the droplets, and spinning them into finger-long spindles to rip the mermaid away. Her limbs shook with the magnitude of the force pulling and yanking at her nerves as the magick tore through her. She waded through the water, trying to get closer, when a boney grip tightened on her shoulder, stopping her in place.

An icy chill pricked her skin as talons pressed deep into her flesh, drawing blood. She called out with a piercing cry. Her gaze darted to the whirling orb of a portal spreading open below. "Get off of me!" Halen swatted the air, shoving the mermaid away.

The mermaid hissed between dagger-pointed teeth. With a whip of her tail, the mermaid lunged. She rolled her shoulders back, tucking her webbed arms to her sides. "I told him you were trouble." She grabbed Halen in her clawed grip.

Halen punched out. She kicked. But she couldn't free herself from the mermaid's grip. She looked for the others.

Pria dragged her brother to the safety of the tunnels. Bloodied shifters lined the ground: arms, legs, and heads attached only by tendons and bone.

The mermaid grabbed Halen by the hair and jerked her into the portal, dragging her into a spinning hell. The portal swirled with an undulating current, whirling her like a rag doll in a washing machine. Above, Dax's limp body spun round and round. Below, the two mermaids rushed toward her, their black lips stained red with murder.

Halen fought to break free, but the more she struggled, the faster the portal spun. The mermaid yanked her against her scaled chest, surfacing, while Dax and the other mermaids drifted away. The night stars peered from above, a prime seat to witness her death.

Halen sunk her teeth into the mermaid's hands. Black blood coated her tongue and spewed it out as she paddled away.

"Where do you think you're going?" The mermaid splayed her fins, and with a slap of her tail, shoved her back under.

Halen drifted,

down,

down,

down.

She clamored to the surface, each stroke a stabbing sword tearing her worn muscles. But when she reached her destination, her hope swelled.

On the shore, Harry, and Faisal guided Boris from the water. Lacelle waded into the lake with Orca and Luke by her side. Catch wasn't far behind.

Halen kicked harder. If she could just make it to land...

A tail slapped the water, the sound reverberating in the night air.

"Halen!" Luke wadded back into the lake.

"No. Go back," she tried to shout, but her voice came out cracked and warbled.

Luke dived beneath the surface.

The mermaid raced beside Halen. "I don't know what Asair sees in you."

Confusion washed over her. *Asair?* She couldn't believe the mermaid had spoken his name. She scooted against the water, gaining a few feet of distance. "Do you know where he is?"

"One dead siren won't open Etlis." The water crackled with ice.

"No, please!" Halen shook her hands, hoping to ignite her magick. "Etlis will open. You can't kill me. You can't let the fires burn through Earth again. Earth needs water and so do you."

"Asair's heart is mine." The mermaid hissed.

"Halen," Luke shouted.

The mermaid's attention shifted to him. Her mouth spread with a twisted grin. A brilliant red light shimmered from between her fingers.

"Don't touch him." Halen kicked, her foot slipping over scales and flesh, but from the heat in her heel, she knew she had hit bone.

The red orb dropped in the water, melting the ice.

"We're done here." The mermaid grabbed Halen by the throat.

"We're connected." Halen sputtered her words between choked breaths. "If you care about Asair, you won't hurt me. He'll hate you."

"He already does." Smoke spewed from her lips, rushing Halen.

The force hit hard, ripping her inside out as if every fiber of her split with the burning smoke. Halen held her hand out to block the next blow. The mermaid grabbed her arm, snapping the bone from wrist to elbow. Halen screamed, but the mermaid tightened her grip. How long would the mermaid play with her prey? She didn't know, but without the elixir, she was helpless to her captor.

The mermaid cried out, and she released her hold.

Behind her, Luke floated with a baton secured in his fist. The weapon rippled in his grip with the energy of the lake. He rose and struck the mermaid.

She wailed with a deafening cry and the water baton dripped into the lake.

"We have to go. Now." He caught Halen by the hand, pulling her against him, and rolled her to his back. "Hold on."

She grasped him tight, and he dived. His body rushed

through the water, steady and rhythmic as if he were one with the beat of nature. The mermaid's eyes glowed with vengeance as she chased them, but even with fins and scales, she was no match for Luke's speed.

They reached the shore, and Harry dragged Halen up by the waist. For a moment, Halen thought they might be in the clear, when a wild wind whipped up from the desert, shoving dirt and grit around them. Halen shielded her eyes, and the others scattered. "Luke!" Her fingers slid past his as she glided in the air.

She winced with the pressure, cutting her breath as hooked claws wrapped around her rib cage. She clawed the night air, struggling for freedom, when a smoky voice spoke from above, "I've got you now."

Halen turned toward the silver wings shimmering against the stars. "Jae." Relief washed through her. The dragon pulled her up over the desert, away from the churning lake and the mermaid's wails.

Luke stood with his gaze cast upward at her, and her heart ached.

"We have to go back for them. We can't leave," she said, but Jae climbed higher, farther and farther away, abandoning Luke and the ones who had fought by her side.

13

"GET HER INSIDE, QUICK!" A girl shouted from the rooftop below. With the wind rushing against her, Halen couldn't bring the person's face into view. She tumbled gently from the dragon's grip onto the roof. Someone scooped her from the ground. Her cheek pressed into a warm shoulder as they walked indoors and into the light.

"I've got you now, darling."

Asair. Her lips parted to speak, but her chattering teeth forbade words to pass. Her body rolled with a quake of shivers, even though heat radiated from the boy holding her.

"Elixir—now!" Asair shouted.

His desperate call whipped panic through her, releasing another wave of shivers. He kicked the door shut, blocking her view of Jae as she ascended into the night sky.

Inside, water pipes lined the ceiling. A buzz flickered to a hum, and a fan whirled, pushing a hot breeze into the air, but fevered chills overtook her.

"Set her down. I'll get Halen out of these wet clothes. Go find some clothes from my room."

Halen knew this voice too, and she wanted so desperately to speak to her sister, to tell her about the others, and that Catch was still alive. "Help them." She pushed the words to her throat.

When Asair set her on the ground, she cried out from the pain of her broken bone. He touched her shoulder, running his fingers down to her wrist. As his magick connected with hers, warmth spread down through to her bones, alleviating the gut-wrenching agony. "They did this to her." His teeth gritted.

"I've got the elixir. I'll take care of her—go. We need Jae in human form now." Natalie seemed to float to the ground, settling on the floor next to her. Halen was sure the fever had spread to her thoughts, making her delusional.

"I won't be long." When Asair's hand left her skin, her arm throbbed.

"What the hell did the mermaids do to you?" Natalie shook her head. Her cool hand rested at the back of Halen's neck, tilting her up. She held the elixir to her lips. "Take it all."

The syrupy liquid slid down her throat, warming her through to the core. At once, the shaking subsided, yet her broken arm ached with fiery pain.

"Catch is alive. We have to help him."

"What? You saw him?" Natalie's eyes widened.

She nodded; the motion blurring her vision. "He's in the desert."

"Oh, hell no," Natalie whispered under her breath. "I'll send help as soon as we get you fixed up."

"There are others." She coughed, rolling to her side.

"We'll find them." She took Halen's arm, then gently blew over the wound, saying, "*Kintalisium.*" As she spoke the word of healing magick, a prickling sensation ran across her flesh, sinking beneath the skin. "That will help with the pain until Jae sets the bone."

"Thank you."

"Hey, this is what sisters do for each other. Well, minus getting you ripped apart by mermaids." Her smile remained tight, but Halen welcomed the sight of her sister all the same. "We didn't have a choice. I'm really sorry."

Natalie's cheeks flushed, her dark hair sat atop her head in a coiled bun, and her green eyes flicked with concern. Halen took in her sister like sunlight on a winter's day; thankful just to be in her presence.

"We have to get you out of these wet clothes." When Natalie removed Halen's shirt, her fingers brushed against her goosebumps. "You have a residue on your skin." She smelled the blue streaks. "Damn shifters. We have to get this off." She waved. "*Criptopoic, Villitus, Gorgorgi.*" A hose floated into the air, and the faucet turned with a squeak. Natalie grabbed the nozzle, aiming it toward her. "This is going to suck, but we have to get the potion off. It may have tracking abilities, but my guess is it dulls your powers."

Halen pinched her eyes tightly when the water sprayed her body. With her already fevered flesh, the water stung, but she didn't care as long as Natalie removed every trace of the owl compound from her skin—though nothing would cleanse her mind of the horrific memories.

The pipes above knocked, then banged with a thud. "*Hectocious!*" Natalie shouted, shutting the water off. The water surrounding them dispersed with a rush of warm air, drying the surrounding concrete. "*Diphillious.*" A blanket floated into the air, and when Halen looked to see where it had come from, she spotted a wheelchair. She glanced to Natalie's legs tucked at her side.

As if sensing her next words, Natalie answered. "I can't feel my legs. Jae's still working on it, but Aurelia's arrow was a gold one. It could be worse." She shrugged. "My soul could be trapped in that cow's arrow."

"I'm so sorry." Halen rose to a sitting position, her head swimming, her stomach churning.

"None of this is your fault," Natalie said.

Halen glanced at the clanging pipes once more. "Where are we?"

"The Hunters' fortress."

"What?" Panic rushed back through her. "After what they did to you?"

"Emil and his sister, Vita, are on our side. We've locked the others out and surrounded the perimeter with Jae's magick. We're safe here—for now."

"We're not safe anywhere." Halen fought back the rising bile. "You didn't see the look in the mermaid's eyes." She felt a drip at the base of her nose, and when she swiped her hand across her mouth, an oily black sludge slicked her fingers.

Natalie gripped her shoulder, tugging the blanket down. "They scratched you, too. Damn mermaids."

"Let me see." Asair stepped into view. His jade gaze wouldn't meet with hers, even though Halen couldn't take her eyes off him. He handed the clothes to Natalie, and he knelt beside her. When his fingers brushed the mermaid's talon marks, she winced. He sighed, his breath hitching as if he were the one in pain.

"I'm okay." She touched his hand, but he withdrew, standing.

"There's nothing okay about this." His fists balled at his sides. His anger twisted inside her, spinning with the mermaid venom. Halen gagged as the black sludge bubbled up her throat.

Natalie grasped her own throat. "Get out of here now. You're not helping."

He shook his head. "I'm so sorry. This is all my fault."

He left before she could beg him to stay.

Natalie wrapped her arm around her shoulders, drawing her in closer. "I've got you."

Halen leaned against her sister. The room spun as exhaustion swept over her. Though she survived the shifters and the mermaids, the battle ahead plagued her mind; without freedom from Dax, her magick would destroy them all. "You need to stay away from me. I'm cursed."

"Don't be ridiculous." When she tugged the blanket back up over Halen, Natalie's touch lingered on her birthmark.

Halen tucked her arm back under the blanket.

"You're burning up." Natalie patted her damp forehead.

"You can you feel my fever?" She met her sister's gaze, though she fought to keep her eyelids open.

"It's nothing." Natalie glanced away.

Halen closed her eyes. "We're sisters. We need to stop lying to each other." She drifted with this thought, unable to bring the next words to her lips, but she wanted to warn Natalie to run. In her presence, no one was safe.

14

"You can't go in there." Natalie butted her wheelchair against the door to Halen's bedroom. "She needs rest, not you filling up her head with thoughts of, well..." She waved her hand from his head to his feet. "You."

"I just want to see her." His heart ached with the thought of her on the other side, so close yet so far away. He felt as if he were trapped back in his dimension, watching her, unable to keep her safe.

"There's plenty of time. Besides, your bond isn't what she needs right now. Your anger didn't exactly help. Your emotions are running too high."

"I'm sorry. I couldn't bear to see her that way."

"She needs time."

He stared at the closed door, hoping she couldn't feel his despair through the oak. "I've done enough damage."

Natalie's tone softened. "None of this is your fault."

"Really?" His gaze slipped to hers. "You and Halen were born to bring me out of that wretched dimension. Your lives have never been your own because of me."

"Stop blaming yourself. You haven't had much control over your life, either."

"I just wish it were different. At least for you and Halen." His gaze dropped to her wheelchair.

"It is what it is, so get off the big-ass guilt trip you're on

92

and move on." She rolled her shoulders back. "We have work to do. Did Jae find the stone? Was there any sign of the others—of Catch?"

"She believes she's located the area where the stone is buried, but there's no point in digging it up until Halen is better."

"And Catch?" she asked.

He turned away from her anxious stare. "They're gone. Jae will continue searching when she goes out. Maybe Halen knows where they were headed." Asair placed his hand on the doorknob.

Natalie shoved him back. "Stay away from Halen."

"Like you stay away from Emil?" He challenged. "I know her better than anyone—better than you."

"That might be true, but if your creepy girlfriends see you with her, then who knows what they'll do. Selene sliced her up pretty good. Not to mention, she broke her arm. If it were up to me, we'd be having sushi tonight."

His gaze narrowed.

"What? Don't look at me that way. They could have killed her."

"They wouldn't kill her." He wrung his hands. He wasn't so sure. Selene's obsession with him clouded her judgment. He wondered how far she would go.

"We need to send them away. Their idea of help is all kinds of messed up. Did you know they killed the shifters?"

"They're no better than the Hunters," he reminded her.

She grasped the wheels, and the chair shook. "No one wants Etlis to open—not even Emil. He may want to break the curse, but he wouldn't. He loves Earth too much. He's on our side."

He glanced at her arm, flecked with needle marks. Natalie's twisted idea of survival worked, but he didn't know for how long. "You can't give them your blood forever. Eventually, they'll thirst for more."

"Emil and Vita haven't killed you, so mind your own business." She shoved her sleeve down.

He sighed. "It's not that I'm ungrateful, but we can't keep this up. We'll have to face Rania, eventually." He placed his hand on the door. "And if the mermaids killed owl shifters, they will come for us as well. We need to leave here."

Natalie's phone buzzed. She slid it out of her hoodie and read the message. "Jae brought the douchebag's heart rate down. Dax is stable."

"I've asked Vita to take out all the water from his room, not even a glass unless one of us is present."

"Then you *are* worried about the mermaids?" Natalie shook the phone.

He raked his hand over his hair. "Kye asked about Dax, but I'll speak to them."

"You do that. You make sure they understand Emil will gut them if they don't comply. Hands off Halen *and* Dax."

"As much as I hate the idea, we still need the mermaids," he said. "They're our eyes outside and they've blocked attacks on the fortress."

"Not for long. Once we get our girl back to normal, we can get rid of them. Between the three of us, we have more power combined." Her phone buzzed again.

"Everything okay?" He leaned over her, hoping to catch a glimpse of the message. Emil had been texting more often, and usually, after she read his messages, she grew quiet.

"Emil needs me." Her gaze darted between the hallway and Halen's door. "Stay out of her room." She wagged her finger. "Remember, I can feel what you're feeling, so if you go in there, I'll know."

He crossed his heart.

She rolled her eyes. "Yeah, right. Just don't wake her. She needs rest. I'll be back in twenty."

As soon as the whir of the wheels of Natalie's chair disappeared, he cracked the door open. A grand forest-green canopy of velvet draped the king-sized four-poster bed, making her seem so small tucked beneath the silk sheets. He stepped inside, peeking down the hall for signs of Natalie, and when he didn't see her, he shut the door. As he walked toward the bed, the glassy eyes of a mounted deer head followed him. Below the deer's head sat a dresser with a blue jay and a smaller marble table adorned with a muskrat, baring its sharp little teeth. Otho's passion for hunting was displayed on every surface. He hated seeing her in this room of death. When he sat on the edge of the bed, Halen let out a soft moan. Her eyes fluttered beneath her lids.

"You're safe," he whispered and her breathing steadied. He brushed the strands of her black hair from her face. As he ran his fingers across her cheekbone, past the dark shadows beneath her eyes, he couldn't help but wonder when she had slept last. She was so brave, fighting even with weakened magick, while he hid in a protected fortress.

A hundred years in a dimension alone hadn't prepared him for the Earth realm. Deciding for others was easy without facing consequences. He was thankful for Quinn's knowledge. For being so young, the siren boy had lived a full life. Sadly, most of his life involved survival. But with Quinn's training combined with his magick, he could survive—but not without her.

He leaned closer, and her breath, sweet with Jae's potion, fanned his face. He kissed her forehead, lingering seconds longer than he should, and as he drew back, her eyes opened. She stared through him, her piercing eyes tugging at his soul. Using every ounce of willpower, he retreated, sitting back with his arms crossed. "Hello."

"Hi." Her mouth spread with a sleepy grin.

"You're looking much better." He matched her smile.

"Don't lie. I look like hell." She shifted, moving her arm, and she let out a sharp breath.

He gritted his teeth, thinking of her battling Selene, but he wouldn't let his rage ruin this moment. "You look like heaven to me." He took her hand up in both of his; a bold move since he had no clue if she hated him for making her leave the forest alone, for sending the mermaids, and for not coming to get her himself.

"Where were you?" Her words were but a whisper. Her hand slipped from his. She tucked it under her pillow and rolled to her side, being careful of her cast. "Did you know I was with the owls? Did you know about Nelia's deal?"

"Quinn's girlfriend made a deal with them?" he asked.

"I thought you would know—she traded me with that necklace; the one Quinn had you give Nelia." Her tone held accusation.

"You don't think I knew she would do this?"

"You do have access to his memories."

He scanned through Quinn's past, finding the necklace; a charm given to him by his father. The same infinity knot was etched along the Hunter's gold arrows. "The necklace has powers," he said, "but I have no clue what it does."

Her eyebrows rose.

"Honestly. I believe if Nelia gave it to them, it was to protect you. I don't think she meant you harm. She probably thought it was the best place to hide. Quinn never betrayed us—he gave his life so I could live."

"The owls are evil. They wanted to chop me up to pieces."

The hairs on his arms rose. "They're collectors of magick. I'm sorry."

"You should have come." Her tone was clipped.

He studied the patterned carpet, afraid to see the

expression written on her face, even though her anger rushed through his veins. "I know, but we can't leave the fortress, not with Rania hunting sirens."

"There are other sirens out there who need our help. Sirens fighting for their lives. If you could have seen what those savage owls did to them, you wouldn't stay here." She pushed off the covers and sat. "We need to fight back."

"And we will, once you're better, but Rania and the Hunters aren't our only problems." He didn't know how to bring up the desert, and the lives she had taken, without upsetting her more, but as long as they were being honest... "Your magick is not your own. What you did in the desert is all over the news." He pumped his fists where the magick flickered to his palms, throbbing with the memory of the dark spells she cast. "Natalie and I felt it first. I didn't want to believe the feelings were true, but Dax has a hold on you."

"Don't you think I know what he made me do?" She gathered her inky black hair in her fist. "It's all I can think of." She held out her hand. "Look at me. Look what I've become."

Her desperation ached in his chest. He never should have pushed her away in the forest. He clenched his fists tighter. He would never forgive himself if she couldn't be free of Dax. Asair knew too well the pain of the bond. He wouldn't wish it on anyone. "We can fix this—I promise. We'll find a way."

"If I have to cut my arm off to be free of him, I will."

"I'm afraid the bond goes deeper than just the physical." He sighed. "But we will start with the silver."

"Where's Dax?" She stepped from the bed and her feet wobbled.

He grasped her waist, guiding her back to the mattress. "Take it easy. He's safe. Dax is receiving the best treatment,

97

and Jae's already working on a way to get the silver out, but we can't try anything until you're one hundred percent. So, you need to rest." He nodded toward the pillow.

"I can't sleep knowing the other sirens and Catch are out there." Her eyes welled with tears, and she swiped them away. "I just left them all behind. They risked their lives for me. I have to do something."

"Help them by getting stronger." He reached for her hand, and she let him take it. He ran his fingers over the marks of dark magick, praying it wasn't too late to save her.

ASAIR'S TOUCH lingered on Halen's skin long after he left the room. Bound by Jae's Circle of Three spell, his anger and fear wound through her. But she didn't know if he was afraid for her life or frightened of her. She twisted a curl of black hair around her finger, the coyote's blood stained in her mind. *Death doesn't let you forget*, Pria's words whispered through her thoughts as she traced the lines of her birthmark.

Her gaze drifted to the door creaking open. "You're awake!" Natalie crossed the room and stopped next to the bed. "How are you feeling?"

Halen propped up with her back against the plush, quilted headboard. "Jae's potion is numbing the pain in my arm." Her gaze drifted to her sister's wheelchair, but she quickly averted her stare.

"Hey," Natalie patted the bed. "I'm not thrilled about the chair, but I'm alive. You have to face the damn thing, otherwise, you're never going to look at me. I'm still the same person. I'm not helpless."

"I didn't say—"

She smiled. "I know, but you're giving me that pitiful look everyone gives me when they see me for the first time."

"I'm sorry."

"Once a kickass siren, always a kickass siren. Plus, check out these spokes. Each one's equipped with a dagger. This one even has a poison tip." She pointed to a dagger with a blood red handle. "I have my own personal arsenal." Her grin broadened with the mirror image of their mother's smile.

Natalie was putting on a brave face. Halen could at least do the same. "It's so good to see you." Halen swung her legs over the bed and wrapped her good arm around her sister.

Natalie held her tight. "I'm the one who should be sorry. We've been hiding out in the fortress. We should have been out there looking for you, not just Jae. We tried a locator spell, and that didn't work. I guess the owls blocked it."

"It's better that you stayed here. It's not safe out there." She sat back. "Elosians attacked the beach house." She left out the part about killing Peter, and she certainly wasn't ready to tell Natalie it might not be safe in the Hunter's fortress either, with Dax dragging her magick to the dark side. She would save the gruesome details for later.

"We've had to keep our magick low-key here. Every time we cast a spell, a new shifter comes sniffing around. The mermaids…" Natalie glanced at her cast. "I'm sorry about what they did to you. We never should have sent them. I should have come for you."

"Thank you." Halen wobbled out of the bed, using the nightstand for balance. "I wouldn't be here if you hadn't."

"Hey, you should be resting. Jae will have my head if you're running about. That cast won't be off for a few days."

"Where is Jae?" Halen headed to the standing mirror. She wore blue plaid flannel pajamas with fuzzy gray socks up to her knees. Her cast wrapped her arm from wrist to elbow, with sprigs of lavender poking through the ends.

"Jae's taking care of Dax. He's stable."

Jae would know what to do—she had to find a way to set her free from Dax. Halen met the glassy gaze of a stuffed coyote guarding the exit. Maybe she wasn't so unlike the Hunters, after all. "What about the Hunters?" Halen headed to the door.

"Only Vita and Emil are here. The others joined the fight."

"And you trust them?"

"With our lives," Natalie said. "And with the fate of Etlis."

Halen grasped the doorknob. "So, it's just us?"

"Where do you think you're going?"

"I have to see it." She opened the door.

"See what?" Her sister's face paled.

She choked back the sudden rush of tears. "I need to see where they died."

Natalie wheeled beside her, her motions so fluid and quick as she shut the door. "Not today."

"You don't understand. I keep playing that day in the hotel over in my mind and everything I did afterward. If I had done one thing differently, held mom longer, confided in Tage, or instead of cowering…" She bowed her head. "I may have saved them. I need to see where they died with my own eyes. I need closure."

"There's nothing we could have done. Tage bled out. The mermaid venom was too strong for her body. If she had been a blue moon siren, we could have saved her. And I tried everything to bring Corinne back. But she wouldn't wake. I have her ashes, Halen. When you're feeling better, we can put Corinne to rest—together."

Halen brushed away the tears. "She was your mother too."

"I know, but I didn't know her. I mourned her a long

time ago. But I'll be there for you. I understand what it feels like to not have a mother."

"I'm sorry you didn't know her. She was incredible." Halen paused, swallowing back the burning grief rising in her throat. "You look just like her."

"And you have her strength." Natalie smiled.

"We both do." Halen brushed her face dry with her sleeve. "My friend was strong, too. Do you have Tage's ashes?"

"Yes, and Quinn's sister, Maddie."

"So, she didn't survive the fire?" Her shoulders slumped with the heavy weight of death. "I thought maybe Jae had saved her."

Natalie shook her head. "They were in different rooms when the fire rings exploded."

"I'm sorry." Halen touched Natalie's shoulder. "I know you cared for her."

"We've all lost ones we love. I'll be damned if we lose any more. We're going to find Catch."

"And the other sirens. Asair wants to wait, but they will need our help." Luke's stricken gaze as Jae ripped her from his grip haunted her. He fought for her without question; she would return the favor.

"We'll find them all, but I have to warn you, the other Hunters are savage. If they've joined with Rania, then I pray your friends have a good place to hide."

"You said only two Hunters are here? Where is Ezra?"

Natalie's face flickered with surprise. "He's not Ezra anymore."

"But he's inside the Hunter. He can speak if he wants to. Their souls aren't merged. The Hunter only stole his body."

"Otho is on the hunt like the others. They're on the same side as Rania. I'm sorry—your friend is gone."

"I see." Her energy waned and her legs shook.

"Why don't you sit back down." Natalie nodded toward the bed.

Even though the bed was the last place Halen wanted to be, she followed her sister's advice. She sat on the plush mattress, running her fingers over her cast. The Hunters had brought so much death to her family and friends. "You know this—us being here—is so messed up, right?"

"We're safe here. Emil won't let them hurt us."

"He couldn't stop them from attacking us in the forest. Your soul could be in an arrow if it wasn't for Jae. We have to protect ourselves. What if the mermaids find us here? Do they know about this place?"

Natalie checked her phone as if she had a message, but Halen noticed the screen was empty of notifications.

"Well, do they?" She pressed her sister.

"They're staying in the reservoir until we can leave."

"Here?" She stood but collapsed back onto the bed. "You and Asair are demented. The mermaid who broke my arm doesn't care if Etlis opens. She only wants Asair. I saw it in her eyes."

"It's not ideal, but trust me, we wouldn't bring you to the fortress if we thought it was dangerous. Asair will handle the mermaids. What we need to do now is get you better, free of Dax, and retrieve the water stone before the owls do."

"They buried the stone with my car. Danik, one of the owls, already tried to touch the stone. I don't think they'll try again. Plus, they're wounded. It will take time for them to recover after what the mermaids did to them."

"Magick speeds healing. Jae thinks they will. Even if they don't know how to use the stone, they could use it to barter. Galadia's wand belongs with you," Natalie said.

"I think it's best where it is right now." Halen pulled out a sprig of lavender from her cast. The brightly dyed stem left her fingers green.

"Because of Dax?" Natalie asked.

She nodded.

"He used to shove me in the dark too and lock away the key. You need to fight back."

"You could just take your bracelet off," Halen said.

"I know it's different, but he's the same Guardian. He has weaknesses too."

"Like?" When Dax guided her magick, she felt chained, watching as the destruction unfolded, and at the same time, a sickening pleasure consumed her.

"I had a different relationship with Dax. We were close in other ways." She studied the deer's head. "You have to find what makes him weak against you."

"I don't know if I want to dig around in his head. He's sick."

"I'll help you," Natalie said. "You don't have to do any of this alone. Asair's here too. He's been worried about you. He blamed himself for forcing you away. The man's been a mess."

"It's not his fault. He did what he thought was best, but I think we need to stick together. We're stronger as one."

Natalie smiled. "Spoken like a warrior."

She gasped as if Pria had spoken the word. Warriors sometimes had to kill, but they also saved lives. So far, the only life she had saved was her own. "We need to protect the stone together. What happens to one of us affects us all."

"Exactly, which means you need to sleep and take some more of whatever Jae brewed up for you." She nodded to the teacup and saucer on the nightstand. "If you feel up to it, have a shower and get dressed." She waved to the bench at the end of the bed. "I don't have much, but I brought you some clothes. I figured you'd want comfy."

"You figured right." She felt at ease around Natalie, even though she barely knew her sister. She wished things had been different, that the Tari hadn't split their family, and they had grown up together.

"The bathroom is through that door. I'll check on you in a bit. Dinner will be ready in an hour. We all eat together. It's kind of like our one moment of sanity in our screwed-up world."

"I thought the Hunters didn't eat. I mean, other than our souls." She couldn't get past her sister trusting them so easily.

"Emil and Vita sit for meals. They do it for Asair and me. They do it to hold on to what they lost. They didn't ask for immortality. If Tarius wasn't looming inside Etlis, then they would gladly open the portal, so they could die." Her tone held an edge of anger.

Halen recalled the magick that flared with her sister's temper. How a door ripped from a frame and how chaos ensued with her scream. Her sister had fought alongside her, but there was still so much she needed to learn about her.

"I'm sorry. I didn't know. But you must understand my position. The Hunters came after me, shot you with an arrow, claimed my friend's body, and let Tage and our mother die. Not to mention, they need our siren souls to stay strong. So, forgive me for being cautious when it comes to dinner plans with immortals compelled by a curse to kill us."

"I have them under control." Natalie shoved up her sleeve, revealing a pattern of faint scars mixed with needle marks edging along her birthmark.

Halen's eyes widened. "What have they done to you?"

"Nothing. A little of my blood each day keeps the compulsion at bay. Like eating a square of chocolate when you're on a diet. Curbs the craving." She shrugged.

"You're joking—right? They're siren killers."

"I know this is hard to understand, but Emil loves me.

He would leave the fortress if he thought he couldn't resist."

"And Vita? Does she love you and Asair too?" She couldn't believe Natalie would be so casual about this. "Do you think she'll love me?"

"She wants the same thing as her brother." Natalie pulled down her sleeve.

"And what exactly is that?" Her sparks flared. All of this was so unbelievable. How could her sister cover for them?

"I'll explain at dinner." Natalie opened the door.

Natalie had enough power in her little finger to demolish the fortress. Perhaps she had Emil wrapped around her finger, too. Still, a curse ruled the Hunters' motives. Was her sister blind? She didn't like it one bit, but Natalie was alive and so was she. Whether the Hunters remained loyal, she would find out soon enough. For now, she had her sister's back. At least the Hunters had kept her safe. "Thank you for bringing me here—for everything."

Natalie shook her head. "Don't thank me yet. We're still in a hell of a big mess."

"We can't just sit here. You know that—right?" She huffed, thinking of the others who still wanted their souls.

"Rest now. If you make it to dinner, we'll talk then." She headed toward the hallway.

Halen met her at the door. "I'm glad we're together. Despite everything happening, I hope we can spend some time as sisters."

"We have a lot to discuss." Natalie's gaze skimmed over her long locks. "I'm sorry about Dax. If I hadn't released him, then maybe things would have been different for you." She pursed her lips.

"We all have regrets, but I don't blame you for anything." Halen smiled. "I'm just happy I get to know you now."

"You are a sappy one." She waved behind her as she wheeled down the hall. But Halen saw the tears well in her eyes before she left. "See you at dinner."

A camera rotated toward Halen as she stepped into the hallway. She quickly jumped back inside, though the camera stayed focused on her. Who sat behind the lens? She wondered. Who had eyes on her?

She slammed the door shut. It seemed she wasn't the only one with trust issues. What did it matter who was watching as long as they were all together? But they weren't complete yet. They still needed Catch and the others. Her thoughts filled with the boy wielding the water baton. He didn't even know her and yet he had risked his life for her. She wouldn't let Luke down. She wouldn't rest until she knew they were safe.

16

"WHAT TOOK you so long to return to the fortress!" Asair fought the sparks, begging to strike the mermaids, rip them from the reservoir, and thrust them into the desert sun.

"We needed to feed." Selene's black lips spread with a mischievous grin.

"You broke Halen's arm!" He balled his fists at his sides, keeping his hands from strangling her. Shadows of her sisters' fins loomed beneath the surface of the water, reminding him he was outnumbered. His magick could unravel worlds, but he didn't know if it would win against the dark spells cast by three demons. With Halen near, he wasn't about to test it.

"I retrieved her from the owls. I warned you lives would be lost." Selene lingered at the edge. Her elbows propped on the concrete.

"Funny how your sisters returned with Dax, and there's not one scratch on him."

She strummed her talons on the concrete, the sound gritting his nerves. When he stepped toward her, she trailed her finger across his sneaker. "I wouldn't have killed her. I just wanted to see if she still had it in her. I don't know why you put so much faith in the siren. I've seen inside her soul. She could defeat Tarius, but she never will. She loves him." Her gaze shot to meet his, catching him unaware.

Before he had a chance to block her, she delved deep inside his emotions, reading how this revelation of Tarius and Halen might affect him. Even though the thought of Halen's past soul still loving Tarius tortured his mind, he never would let Selene see. "Galadia left Tarius for a reason. Besides, we both know the soul's nature is strongest in the present life. The past has little influence." He didn't know this for sure, but just stating it as fact helped him digest the horrible thought; Halen might love the enemy.

Jae had warned that if Dax and Halen were insepara-ble, then something would have to be done to contain Halen. Eventually, she would wean off the elixir, but with the silver inside her, her magick would never truly be her own. With a monster after her soul and one chasing her heart, her magick wouldn't have a chance. Jae worried the circle of three was tainted already.

"You better hope she doesn't love him, or we're all in trouble." Again, she tested, poking an open wound to see if any of her words hurt. "Or do you think she might love you instead?"

"Don't be ridiculous. You've seen inside my head. You know how I feel about Halen."

Selene wagged her finger. "You would sacrifice yourself for her—I call that love. You shared each other's souls. She's seen all of you and you all of her... Every lifetime. This is more powerful than the physical time you've spent together. Look how we're bonded. How our love spanned a hundred years, and yet we have barely seen one another." Her tone sounded hopeful.

Naivety had blinded him from fully understanding the complicities of a curse when he had forced her into an alliance. "You've been loyal, Selene. Even when my heart stopped and the curse broke." He knelt near the water, but not too close.

When he had summoned them to the fortress, he had

realized quickly what he had thought was his command was actually her wish. She convinced her sisters to stay and protect him, but Kye and Diya didn't care for him the way she did. Selene had wanted him long before his blood had turned her into a water demon. She was the one who convinced the others to drink his blood. She pledged her loyalty, her heart—her soul. Now she expected Asair to do the same.

"It's time you choose me. You owe me." She slapped her fins against the water. "I will protect you. Halen has the Hunters and her sister. She doesn't need you."

"I'm bound in the circle of three. I can't fight Jae's spell."

"Then what better reason to part? How silly would it be if Rania found all three of you together? How long do you think the Hunters can shield you from their brothers and sisters? If you were wise, you would let Natalie's Hunter boy spear her heart. He could keep her soul safe in his arrow. If you truly don't want Etlis to open, let the Hunters protect both sisters."

Her smile now cut through him. If Dax couldn't be separated, would this be Halen's fate? No, he couldn't allow this idea to bloom. "This is not an option."

"I've overheard the whispers. This is what Natalie wants. She's practically begged Emil to take her soul. She knows what's best for the realms. Natalie may convince her sister to do the same. Come with us before they trap you— be with me."

Was it true? Or another one of Selene's games? They had discussed this option once but had decided against it. Natalie couldn't possibly think they were better off in the Hunters' arrows. She had fought for her life, begging Jae to save her from a fate within the gold rod. No, Natalie wouldn't betray them this way. But the mysterious text messages and her shifting mood hinted otherwise. "I can't leave."

"You can't, or you won't?" She slammed her fist down, splitting the fissures he had created even wider.

He dared not meet her furious gaze.

"If I allow the shifters to pass through the next portal, you won't have a choice. Why don't we call in Natalie and the Hunters—let's take a vote."

"You wouldn't." She would. She had protected him, but Halen's presence only fueled her dark rage.

"Kye wants the Guardian boy. Hell, if I know why." She waved her hand dismissively. "But the twin sirens are nothing to me."

Even if he went with her, Natalie and Halen would still be tracked. "We need to stop Rania first."

"Rania? I'm not going near that foolish Elosian, and neither will you. Besides, it's Halen's head she wants."

"Don't forget. This was Rania's son's body." He touched his chest where Quinn's heart beat. "We'll never be free. Rania wants us all. This has to stop now."

She shook her head. "I'll consult with my sisters about Rania, but you must decide. I'm not going after that Elosian and her Krull army until you choose me."

He bowed his head. He had vowed when he found Halen that he wouldn't place her in further danger. Leaving was the only way. Selene wouldn't hurt him, and the portal would remain sealed.

Her determined glare locked with his.

This wasn't a negotiation he would win, and he feared she would take the offer off the table if he waited to answer. He nodded, turning away. "We'll leave tonight."

17

Halen dangled her feet over the bed, her toes barely touching the wood floor. She ran her hand along the velvet drapery, admiring the plush décor. The mounted animal heads with their glass eyes brought back memories of the desert, while the Renoir reminded her of all she had lost.

She hopped off the mattress, approaching the painting slowly as if the subject might leap from the wall. One day, Halen hoped to capture such beauty in her sketchbook. Art school was the dream, but not now. Maye, never.

She thought of the other sirens hiding in the desert. Their dreams turned to nightmares with Danik and Pria's experiments. Had they found a safety? Or were they still running? She hated herself for hiding in the Hunter's fortress, protected behind concrete walls and surrounded by priceless paintings.

Halen caught her reflection in the standing mirror, her dark hair mocking her for her sins in the desert. She gathered the strands and twisted them back with one hand. Already, her heart was heavy enough without the reminder. Perhaps this was her weakness—feeling too much. Dax harnessed her emotions so easily. She had to toughen up, so he had nothing left to manipulate.

A knock on the door sent her pulse racing. She spun on her heel, and her breath quickened. She wasn't ready to face the Hunters on her own. She rushed across the room, wedging the door open.

"What's wrong?" Natalie glanced up at her.

"Nothing…" She peered behind her sister for signs of the Hunters.

"Well, you look much better." Natalie's tight smile said otherwise.

"You're lying, but I'll take it."

"Do you feel like eating yet? Because Stephan made chocolate mousse. It's amazing."

Again, the guilt of having so much when the others had nothing tore through her. "You have a chef? Is that a good idea? How can you trust him?"

"We keep a staff of ten—marked by Vita or Emil."

Dax bore the Hunter's mark etched along his forearm. Otho had marked him to track her down using the Guardian connection against Dax. It hadn't ended well. And she always feared if Dax woke, Otho would use the mark to control him once more. "And you trust the Hunter's mark?"

"Absolutely, plus we added one other…" She coughed into her sleeve, turning away. "So, are you hungry?"

"Um, yeah, but you were about to say something," Halen said.

"Nope." She shook her head, her eyebrows raising.

Halen touched her shoulder. "Look, you can't protect me with secrets anymore. We have to be straight up with each other. I need to know everything."

"You're right. I just wanted to give you a little time to adjust to all this. The fortress can be overwhelming at first." She wheeled forward, and the camera followed.

Halen shut the door behind her. "Are the cameras necessary?"

"We need as many eyes as possible right now. I know

113

they're a pain in the ass. Believe me, the last thing I need to be recorded is Emil sneaking into my room at night."

"So, it's not all doom and gloom around here." She nudged her sister, smiling.

"Let's just say, I'm happy cameras aren't recording *everything*."

"At least you're happy." She meant it, though she had to admit a part of her was a little jealous. With the burden of the water stone and Dax meddling with her magick, happiness was a long way away.

"I don't know what I would do without Emil. He understands me." Natalie continued down the hall. "And his sister? She can resist on a little of your blood as well?" Halen didn't quite share the same confidence they wouldn't try to spear her.

"Vita has more self-control than all of them."

"Yeah, but when I faced the Hunters in the forest, they didn't look a year over twenty. Some sirens weren't as fortunate. Did you know they built the fortress because a lot of sirens used to be in this area? They moved here to kill."

Natalie glanced out the stained glass picture window.

In contrast to the interior, which was adorned with marble statues, crown molding, and grand crystal chandeliers, the fortress's exterior was a bleak shield of concrete and glass. The comforts didn't fool Halen—somewhere horrible crimes took place in hidden rooms and prison cells where her mother died and Tage bled to death.

"They aren't perfect." Her words were clipped.

"Hey, I'm sorry. I just have a hard time understanding how a siren ended up loving a Hunter. Or how it's even possible? Isn't he ancient?"

"He is." She laughed. "But we've found a bond that surpasses this lifetime." She broke her gaze from the window and continued down the hall.

"So, you really love him?"

"When Aurelia captured me, she wanted to learn my powers and the spells Lina taught me."

"Lina?" Tasar had once mentioned that Natalie and Lina had been close, but that Natalie had abused her powers.

Natalie shook her head. "Lina taught me spells only Etlins should cast. Only when Dax abandoned me in the seam, I craved a new power. I cast some spells I'm not very proud of." She gathered her hair to the side.

Halen nodded, understanding their identical hair color was more because of magick than genes.

"Aurelia's been trying to find a loophole around the Hunter's curse. She's searching for a way to live even after Etlis opens." She bowed her head. "I couldn't help her, so she chained me in a cell and left me to rot."

"Emil saved you?"

"Emil and Vita aren't like the others. He set me free and protected me from his sister. He's a good person."

"Our mother is dead because of them." She couldn't get past this.

"We came for you in the hotel to protect you from the Tari. No one wants the portal to open, but no one wants to spend eternity in flames, either. The earth is still so fragile. We have to work together."

They passed a row of oil paintings of the Hunters poised for battle. Her sparks flickered when she met the painted stare of the boy Lina had turned to stone—the boy whose soul now inhabited Ezra's body. "Where did they keep mom?"

"In the cells," Natalie all but whispered.

"And where are the mermaids?" Her arm ached just asking.

"The reservoir. It's cramped, so they're a little testy."

"Yeah, I know." She lifted her cast.

"Selene would do anything for Asair," Natalie said.

"Stay away from the reservoir, and really, until this whole thing is over, you should avoid Asair. Let him work things out with them."

"He needs to let the mermaids go. We're better off without them."

"I agree, but Asair feels obligated to them."

"Like he does to me."

"That's different. He cares for you."

"He feels guilty. If I can feel it, I'm sure you can too. His guilt is one of his weaknesses," Halen said.

"It's all of ours," Natalie said.

Voices filled the hall as they approached the dining room. Her sparks flickered when she spotted the two Hunters at the table. Their complexions were smooth, with plump, rosy cheeks as if they had killed seconds before her entering. When Emil stood to greet her, she stopped still as a deer sensing footsteps in the forest.

"It's okay," Natalie urged. "They won't hurt you."

Flashes of gold arrows cutting through the trees and her hands slick with her sister's blood plagued her thoughts.

"Welcome." Emil remained standing until Natalie was by his side. He kissed her cheek, then took the place to her left.

The Huntress stood. She wore a royal blue silk top tucked in on one side of her black leather pants, a holster of daggers at her hip. "I'm Vita. We met in the forest. We mean you no harm. Please join us."

Halen searched the faces for Asair and Jae, but two empty place settings remained.

"Jae is still hunting." Natalie looked to Emil. "Where's Asair?"

"I haven't seen him. He's probably still with the sea witches," Emil said.

"You can sit by your sister." Vita shifted to the seat across and sat.

Halen swallowed the hesitation clawing at her throat. Each step she took felt like a lock fastening in a trap, but she wanted to make this work. At least for Natalie, she would try. She sat with her hands folded in her lap, sparks trailing her fingertips.

A young man with a red goatee tied with a little green ribbon at the tip entered the dining room. He balanced a large silver tray on his shoulder. Her gaze darted to the thick scar forming a cross along his forearm. *Marked.* She inhaled a sharp breath. Even though Natalie mentioned he wouldn't harm her unless the Hunters commanded him to do so, she didn't trust the arrangement.

Natalie leaned close, whispering, "Breathe. He's compelled to obey."

Obey who? She didn't think he would follow her command. But if he was a threat, her sister showed no concern. Still, Halen couldn't shake the feeling that danger loomed, watching, waiting for the perfect moment to pounce.

The young man served Vita first, setting the china plate overflowing with a stuffed filo pastry, roasted potatoes, green beans, and carrots in front of her. Even though Halen's gut turned with suspicion, the meal smelled delicious. He then served Emil, then Natalie, and Halen last. Hunters first, then sirens, Halen noted. It was clear where his allegiance fell.

"Will master Asair be joining us this evening?" He stared longingly at Asair's empty chair as if his absence pained him.

"We're not sure." Vita waved, then stabbed a carrot with her fork. "Please keep his meal warm in the kitchen."

He nodded and headed back through the door.

"I swear Asair's blood is stronger than our mark." Emil snorted as he stuffed a roasted potato in his mouth whole.

Natalie elbowed him.

"What? If she can't handle the truth, then she'll never face Tarius." His dark gaze slipped to Halen. "She held her own with those creepy owls. That's something."

"That's the second measure, isn't it?" Halen shoved the plate away. "The staff drank Asair's blood."

"Eat." Natalie nudged her. "We had to be extra sure no one would go rouge on us. It's just a safety precaution."

Halen recalled the desire that overcame her with the taste of Asair's blood. She would have given him the world, each planet, and star in every galaxy and beyond. "Your entire staff is in love with him?"

"I think they would be even without his blood. He's quite the charmer." Vita glanced up from her plate. A soft smile played on her lips. She was a marble sculpture come to life, perfect and stunning in every way. Even her scarlet hair draped over her shoulders in soft waves, not one strand out of place.

"Eat up, Halen." Natalie broke the awkward silence. "Vegetarian, I'm afraid, but it's still tolerable." She cut into her pastry, releasing the steam.

Halen ran the fork over the potatoes, hunger no longer on her mind. How could Asair allow them to drink his blood? Did he really think having the entire staff swoon over him was a solution? Would they also try to attack her like the mermaids?

"There's been a development." Vita swished the wine in her goblet and took a sip before speaking again. "How much have you told your sister?" Her gaze rested with Natalie.

Natalie patted her napkin on her lips. "We haven't had much time to talk. I think it's best if we wait a day or two."

"We don't have a day or two." Vita waved, and a young

woman, who Halen hadn't even noticed before, stepped forward.

She wore the same crisp uniform as the other server, yet her top stretched tight over her curves. Her long ebony hair was woven in a braid; her shimmering gaze skimmed Halen as she poured more wine for

Vita.

This goddess loved Asair, too. Halen clutched her fork. "I may look beat up, but I'm fine inside. You don't have to hide the truth from me. I can handle it."

Vita eyed her as she sipped her wine. "Good. We need action, not little mice running from the cats. Rania was spotted on the Californian coast. This is too close. Now that you are reunited, I say we act now."

"She can't touch us out there." Emil huffed.

"No, but if a shifter helps spin a portal, then it might be a different story. Our reservoir is full of saltwater now, thanks to Asair's pets. She could easily penetrate our fortress."

"Asair won't let that happen. The mermaids listen to him." Natalie's hand shook as she reached for her water goblet.

"Are you so sure?" Vita tilted her glass toward Halen's cast.

Natalie pursed her lips.

Vita continued. "Let's just say, for a moment, Asair didn't have control, and the mermaids decided to let Rania in. Our sanctuary would be your tomb."

"Vita's right. We should go to California." Halen shifted in her seat. "We can't sit here eating while others are fighting for us. We have to defend our own lives instead of letting others die for us. I won't live like this."

"Well said." Vita toasted the air.

"We can't." Fear flecked Natalie's voice.

Had her sister grown too comfortable in the fortress?

Had she lost her edge to fight? This wasn't a time to hide. "How else do we stop Rania? She won't expect us to come to her."

"She has an army." Emil placed his hand over Natalie's.

"And we have the magick of three blue moon sirens." Halen smiled.

"Brilliant idea." Asair entered the dining room and took the seat across from her.

He looked worse for wear, his button-down shirt untucked and his eyes puffy; not a siren who possessed the force of nature at his fingertips. She regretted her suggestion to take him from the fortress.

"The element of surprise has won many battles. I agree with Halen; we stop hiding," Asair said.

The young woman was at his side within seconds, filling his goblet and placing his napkin over his lap. She leaned in close, her bosom brushing his arm. He met her dark gaze and smiled.

Halen knew that look all too well. Even in this new body, she spotted his intention just the same. She had seen the same look in his orb when he toyed with her. "We can't risk your lives." Emil's stern tone broke her from her jealous thoughts. "The portal must remain closed. If you die, then Rania will be the least of our troubles."

"I'm not suggesting we all go." Asair waved the woman away, then folded his hands on the table. "Just me."

"You're not going anywhere alone." Halen's voice cut with anger.

"I'm not going alone." His gaze narrowed. "I'm taking the mermaids."

"I like it." Emil jabbed another potato, then stuffed it in his mouth. "Best plan so far."

"I hate to see your other plans because this one is tragic." Halen glanced at her sister, but she wouldn't meet her gaze. "I'm the one who can touch the water stone. Together, we can end Rania."

"And you're the one Tarius wants." Asair tapped the table. "Besides, we don't have the stone, and you're not free of old Daxy boy. You don't have a handle on your magick. You're out of control."

She ground her teeth, her anger flaring. She couldn't believe he was speaking to her this way. "Are you serious? While you're all playing house and eating meals to feel 'normal,' I've been running for my life. Light or dark, my magick is the only thing that saved me—saved us. Magick is the only way to stop Rania."

"You're thinking of those sirens again. You don't have a debt to them." His tone held a challenge.

"They were there for me—Catch is my friend." The dishes rattled with her rising tone. "I can't just blow off everyone. At some point, being born a blue moon siren has to mean something." She stood, her sparks trailing her arms. The glasses slid along the table.

Vita grabbed her goblet, shooting Natalie a pointed stare.

Natalie grasped Halen's wrist and a calm wave of magick rolled up her arm, cooling her sparks. "Let's not fight. Please sit. Catch was my friend, too. Believe me, I want to do all I can to help. We all do."

Venting wouldn't gain her the Hunters' trust, but with them sitting so calmly, she just wanted to scream. She didn't understand how Asair and Natalie suppressed their magick. She wanted to blow the room to smithereens.

Natalie tugged her down to her seat. "If Jae doesn't see your friends on her next scan, we'll use a locator spell."

"No magick." Vita wagged her finger. "We don't want unwelcome guests."

"A locator spell is simple," Natalie said. "I'll do it to put everyone's mind at ease. Please, Vita."

121

"Fine, but not more than one spell for your friend, Catch. Besides, if he's running with sirens and my brothers and sister are tracking them, I'm afraid they're already dead."

Halen clenched her fists beneath the table, fighting back the sparks as Vita's stern, accusing stare cut through her, the gold arrow not far from her thoughts. She turned to Natalie. "Please try."

"I'll do the spell if you tame your magick," Natalie said.

"I will. Just please find them."

"Stay away from dark magick." Asair shot Halen a pointed stare, even though he spoke to Natalie.

"Then you should stay away from the mermaids." Halen fought the sparks rising with frustration. "They're dangerous."

"They aren't the only ones." Asair's gaze slid to her locks of black hair trailing over her shoulders.

"It must be terrible." Vita held her goblet out for the server to refill. "To be bound to a monster."

Halen recalled all too well the torment of harboring Asair's soul. Her hot gaze fell on the siren boy making her sparks boil. "You have no idea."

18

HER WORDS HURT, but he deserved Halen's scorn. He was a monster for hiding, for not being strong enough to face Tarius.

Halen stood, her furious gaze burning through him. "Thank you for dinner, but I'm not feeling as well as I thought." She spoke between gritted teeth.

Asair knew how she ground the left side harder than the right; he recalled every detail of being in her body. He woke some nights feeling as if his soul were still inside her, only to vanish when he met Quinn's rugged reflection.

"I'll come with you." Natalie wheeled back from the table.

"No." She placed her hand on her sister's shoulder. "I can find my way. I'm fine, really. I just need to rest."

When she passed by him, her magick sparked, and he felt the punch in his gut. He didn't dare glance her way, fearing he would follow—sealing her fate with Selene.

"You didn't have to be such a jerk." Natalie shot him one of her death-ray glares.

He leaned forward, lowering his voice. "I have to get them out of here—now."

"The mermaids?" Emil sipped his wine.

He waited for the server to finish clearing the plates and set the desserts before them before he continued. Even with his blood coursing through the young man's system, he couldn't trust anyone right now. "Selene's restless. She's jealous of Halen."

"We should leave." Vita dragged her spoon across her chocolate mousse. "We can go after Rania. We'll resolve two problems at once. Jae will come too."

"We can't leave the fortress vulnerable." Emil glanced at Natalie; his gaze filled with longing.

Natalie touched Emil's cheek. "Together, Halen and I are unstoppable. You know what I can do—she can do ten times more with the stone."

"That's what I'm afraid of. Is no one going to mention her hair? We all know what it means. She can't be trusted with Dax roaming around her seam." Emil pushed his dessert aside.

"We've all done something horrible at one time or another to survive." Natalie dropped her hands to her lap. "Halen was alone. Her magick protected her and that's what's important."

"If she comes face-to-face with darkness—real darkness—she will embrace it." Emil shook his head. "I see death in her eyes. She's no different from us now." His concerned gaze met with Vita. "I'm staying here with Natalie."

Vita nodded. "I would expect you to, brother." She turned to Asair. "When do you want to leave?"

"Tonight. The mermaids are ready." Asair stood. "But I need to prepare a few things first. I'll meet you at the reservoir."

"I can be ready in an hour," Vita said.

"Please tell Halen goodbye for me," he said to Natalie.

"You should tell her yourself. Don't leave her like this. You'll just make things worse."

"The less time I spend near Halen, the better," Asair

said. "Selene is too unpredictable. I don't know what she'd do…"

"Fine, I'll let her know," Natalie said. "But she won't be happy."

"Wait until I'm gone. It will be easier this way." She would hate him, but he couldn't bear the thought of telling her.

"Stay safe." She reached over, offering her hand.

He leaned across the table, taking her hand in his, and her magick charged up his arm. "I'll be fine." He sighed.

"I'll be able to feel it." She managed a weak smile.

"I wouldn't do anything to put us in danger. It will be worse if I stayed."

"Let him go," Emil said.

She slipped her hand from Asair's, and he turned, forcing back the tears of leaving her. They hadn't spent long together, but he admired her greatly. The Windspeare sisters were unforgettable.

He strode down the hall, his pace slow, not ready to face Selene and her sisters. Once he left, he could never return. He turned toward his bedroom, but he froze in place. His breath quickened when he found Halen lingering in the library.

She stood with her back to him, her head tilted toward the sky of flowers painted on the domed ceiling of the library. It was strange to be so close to her, yet so far away, and it stirred memories of watching her from his dimension. Only then, she was just a girl. Now she was a young woman with a world of magick at her fingertips.

She was a force of nature—both calm and tumultuous. She reminded him of the artic poppy; a flower that blossomed with soft yellow petals, always turning toward the sun, thriving, even when blustery winds and permafrost threatened to rip it from the earth. Though rooted in turmoil, Halen blossomed.

He leaned against the wall, remembering how alive he had made her feel seeing the world through her eyes. He remembered her optimism, her forgiveness, and how easily her heart loved.

"It's not polite to stare." She did not turn to face him.

"I was just heading to my quarters."

Her silence stung.

"Well, goodnight then." He placed his hand on the doorknob. With her so close, his magick flecked his skin with goosebumps. If they were standing in front of Selene now, the witch would snap her bones. Halen wasn't safe with him nearby. He opened the door and no sooner had he opened it than it slammed shut in his face, shoving him back.

He swallowed hard as she stepped forward.

"I used magick in ways I'm not proud of, but I was being hunted. Do you know how many shifters I've murdered?" Her gaze narrowed, the green glinting with her sparks. "And it's tearing me up inside."

He parted his lips to speak when she rushed toward him, her movements so quick he didn't even see her feet move. The idea she could be this in control of her magick both excited and terrified him.

"You don't know what it's been like for me. You have no clue!" She grew more beautiful with each angered breath, like a perfect storm before the first drop of rain.

This is how he should leave her: furious with him, so angry she would welcome his departure, but he couldn't hurt her anymore. "I'm so sorry. I hid in the fortress when I should have been out there looking for you." He should stop now. Close his mouth and go. But he couldn't leave without her forgiveness. "If I could rewind the past, I would have faced Tarius. Then you would be free."

The camera rotated to face them.

She glanced up, and with a flick of her finger, she

opened the door, edging him inside his room. With a wave of her hand, the door slammed behind her.

His pulse raced. "Please forgive me."

"Forgive you." She guffawed. "I'm the one who needs forgiving." She bowed her head. "I'm the monster now."

"We're all the same." He brushed her cheek, then slipped his hand to the nape of her neck, tugging her closer. Her hands flattened on his chest; her electric sparks wound through his heart, connecting with his pulse.

She stepped back. "Everything is so messed up. I was stupid to think that by driving away from the ocean, none of this would follow me." She laughed. "You know, for a moment, I thought I could put everything behind me and start over. I wish I could wake up and be someone else—someone without blood on her hands."

"I understand."

"Do you?" The anger returned to her voice. She held her hands to the air, the bluish tinge of dark magick staining her palms. "Every minute, I think of the shifters I killed. Every second, I crave the power I harnessed that night. I'm starving, and the only way to feed the hunger is more death."

"This is not you. It's Dax. Jae will find a way to separate you." He glanced at her silver birthmark, noticing the dozens of slash marks.

"That's right. That's all of them—every soul I took." She pushed her sleeve down. "It might be too late for Jae to help me. Even if she finds a way to separate Dax, my magick is different."

"You're the same girl. I feel it in here." He thumped his chest. "Jae will find a way. Don't give up hope."

"I need you," she said, her eyes pleading. "I need you and Natalie by my side. I can't do this alone. You know what it's like to be caught up in the Guardian bond. You also know what it's like to be free."

He cast his gaze to the floor, not sure how to tell her he was leaving.

"Asair! Promise me—we stick together this time—we fight side-by-side."

"I will always do what's best for you." He forced a smile to his face.

"No." She met his gaze, her stare penetrating. "Promise me."

"I can't." He led her to the edge of the bed, pulling her by his side. "I have to leave."

"Not without me." She stood. "You can't be serious?"

As he glanced at her cast, thoughts of Selene snaked into his mind. He shouldn't be here now. "I have to go with the mermaids. Rania's close. We'll stop her. Isn't that what you wanted? Then I can look for your friends."

"And you think I can't help?"

"We can't take the risk. Together, we're a target. Natalie and I had some close calls as well." He rubbed his arm where a lion shifter had sunk its teeth before he had summoned the mermaids. "It hasn't been all puff pastry and chocolate mousse."

"I know. I'm sorry I lost it at dinner. I'm not the only one who wants to forget." She sat back down, running her fingers along his scar. "What happened here?"

"Hunters chased us from the forest. We had to stay the night in a city dumpster."

"Now I'm really sorry for what I said." Her face broke with a soft smile, and the ache in his heart eased.

"A shifter found us and tried to eat my arm."

"Shifter bites hurt. It's like they have fire in their teeth." The scar warmed with her touch. "Under my cast is a nasty bite wound from a coyote."

"We've all lost so much. I don't plan on losing you," he said. "I want this to be over. I want you to have the life you should have had."

"You still think I'm this scared little girl. I'm not afraid anymore."

"That's what frightens me." Without fear, she had no boundaries. No measure to pull her away from darkness. Being fearless, Halen wandered both sides of her seam, but with Dax guiding her, the shadows would comfort her like home.

"You think I'm dangerous, then?" Her eyebrows rose.

"I know with Dax as your Guardian, your magick is unpredictable. I understand this more than anyone."

"Because of Elizabeth."

"Yes. After her head injury, she played with my magick. I did some horrible things too."

"Then wait. You said Jae can take the silver out." She waved her arm. "At least wait until I'm free of him. Then we'll fight together."

He wanted nothing more, but he owed Selene. "I need to leave with the mermaids."

"Stay with me." Her voice held no tone of desperation. Her plea sounded more like a demand than a request.

"We need to think of the realms. The mermaids will protect me. Natalie will guide you through." His fingertips sparked as he slid his hand over hers, his magick a wave crashing to her shore.

The ceiling crackled with the sound of magick, and he withdrew his hand. Fissures spread like roots along the ceiling, electrifying with charges of white light.

"What is it?" Halen jumped off the bed.

"You need to leave." He pushed her toward the door, but she held fast.

His sparks surged as water pipes burst, popping, and squealing with the release of pressure while a murky-gray swirling circle spread across the ceiling.

"What are you doing with *her*?" Selene's vengeful hiss filled the bedroom.

"Asair's staying with me." Halen widened her stance.

Selene cackled with chilling laughter. Kye and Diya appeared by her side. "It's time to go, Asair. Choose, or we'll decide for you." Selene shot a whirling ball of smoke toward Halen.

Halen thrust her hand outward, catching the smoke orb, then hurled it back before it exploded.

Asair gasped. Her magick was stronger than he had ever imagined. And he didn't know if it was Selene or Halen that scared him most at this moment.

"Well, you're feeling better." Selene cocked her head.

"Leave her alone. We have a deal." He stepped in front of Halen.

"And it looks to me like you've broken your promise." Flames shot from her fingertips, igniting the bedding.

He spun, blowing with a forced breath, and extinguishing the inferno. "I'll go with you."

"No!" Halen grabbed his arm, her magick hot on his skin. "We can fight them."

He grasped her by the shoulders. "We need the mermaids. Let them stop Rania. Keeping Etlis sealed is our duty." Her face flushed with rage, tears streaming down her cheeks. "I'm so sorry." He kissed her forehead.

Selene reached down, grabbing him in her bony fist.

"Asair!" Halen screamed. The mirrors cracked, and the walls split with her anger. "Don't do this."

He'd sworn when he found her, he'd never leave her side again, but this was the only way to protect her. The mermaids would always want his heart. This was the price of his spell so many years ago. He nodded to Selene, and with a snap of her webbed fingers, the portal shut, leaving Halen and his heart in ruin.

19

"ASAIR!" Halen reached for the ceiling, where only moments ago a swirling portal filled the center.

Emil shoved open the bedroom door, waving his dagger. "What happened?" He scanned the wreckage: the burned bed, the cracked room, the broken girl.

"He's gone!" Halen shook her fist. "Asair left with the mermaids."

Natalie pushed past Emil and wheeled beside her. "He knows what he's doing."

"He thinks I need protection. I can handle the mermaids." Natalie's gaze drifted to her cast.

"That was different. I used a ton of magick to…"

Repeating out loud the events of the massacre and the attack on the owls ripped open too many stitches. "I didn't have elixir. I was vulnerable."

"And it could happen again." Emil sheathed his blade at his hip.

He grasped Halen's shoulder, his touch sending a shiver through her. "You need to gain control. This is exactly what Asair was talking about. This is why you need to stay here."

She didn't trust the Hunter. Her sister may love him, but she couldn't deny the curse compelled them to hunt sirens. For all she knew, he would take her soul while she slept.

She shrugged off his hand. "I'm going after Asair. He can't take Rania on by himself."

"It's too dangerous." Emil's concerned gaze fell on Natalie.

"She's right." Natalie shrugged. "We can't hide here forever. Now that we've lost the mermaids' protection, your brothers and sister will come. So will the shifters."

"I'll speak with Jae. We need a stronger spell over the fortress." He kissed the top of Natalie's head. "I need to let Vita know Asair left." Emil nodded toward Halen and departed.

Halen followed him into the hallway, searching for the direction of her room. She stared at the library where Asair had found her standing beneath the canopy of painted flowers. She wished now that she had fought the mermaids harder. Casting dark magick had to be better than this emptiness consuming her now. But Asair didn't want her to follow. No one trusted her powers, and that hurt just as much.

"I know you care for Asair," Natalie said, breaking the silence, "but listen to me very carefully; the other Hunters will use him to get to you. You have to let him go."

"Like I said at dinner, the three of us can stop Rania —together."

"Then what?"

"What do you mean?"

"It doesn't stop with Rania. We'll be looking over our shoulders for the rest of our lives. What if you die? You're the only one who can get to Tarius. You're the one he wants. Galadia is his weakness. Right now, he's locked away, and he'll remain that way as long as our souls live. We need to consider our options; the Hunters might be right."

"What are you saying?" She spun to meet her.

"The portal will never open if our souls are in the Hunters' arrows. Galadia's soul, your soul, will always be safe."

"You can't be serious. Is this what Emil wants?" After witnessing Natalie's magick, she couldn't believe she would give it all away, and to a Hunter no less. "I knew they couldn't be trusted."

"Emil never wanted immortality. He would love the curse broken, but he also loves this realm. Let me show you something." She headed into the library.

"I need to find Asair." Halen inhaled the smoky residue of the mermaid spell. His departure fueled the rage rolling along her seam.

"Come with me first. This won't take long." Natalie crossed the library and through another entranceway.

Halen followed though she knew nothing Natalie showed her would persuade her to let a Hunter capture her soul.

The hall narrowed, the ornate molding giving way to bare concrete. At the end of the hall, Natalie stopped at a service elevator. She pushed a round yellow button. When the doors slid open, she entered.

Halen stopped short. Each second that passed, the mermaids dragged Asair farther away. "Now's not a good time for a tour."

"Come on. You wanted to know everything. You need to see this. If you still want to go after Asair, if you want to find Catch and the other sirens, I'll go with you, but please let me just show you this first." With a heavy sigh, Halen entered.

Natalie punched in a five-digit code and at once, the elevator rushed down, leaving her stomach on the top floor. Without illuminated numbers specifying exactly how many floors down they were traveling, the whir of the descent panicked her already racing heart.

When she bent over to steady her breath, Natalie grasped her arm. "Are you okay?"

Halen nodded, fearing if she opened her mouth, the few bites she had for dinner would end up on the floor.

The elevator came to an unexpectedly smooth stop. When the doors parted, the scents of jasmine, damp soil, and freshly cut grass filled her lungs. She glanced up.

Beyond, men and women in puffy white suits shifted hoses, adjusting the water spray, so the droplets hit the palm leaves, bending toward the artificial light.

Natalie exited the elevator, but Halen pressed her back against the wall. She counted a staff of three—three new people she couldn't trust.

"They won't hurt you. They would die to protect us. No one here is marked or sipped Asair's blood. They love the Earth realm. They understand what would happen if we died."

"What is this place?" Halen stepped forward, her heels on the edge of the elevator, the toes of her sneakers touching grass. She shielded her eyes from the blinding light.

"Here." Natalie handed her a pair of sunglasses. "Our eyes can't filter this light. You need to wear these."

Halen slipped on the sunglasses, which when worn, cast a soft violet hue to the garden.

"Emil and Vita spent many years working on this project. All our food in the fortress comes from here. We're living in a completely sustainable environment, right in the middle of the desert. Solar energy powers the lights. The water is filtered and recycled." She pointed beyond the grass to a layered planter overflowing with fruits and vegetables reaching toward the ceiling. At the bottom, water trickled through a mound of sand. "The sand works as an insulator and filter at the same time."

"This is incredible. How long has this garden been here?"

"They started back when the portal weakened when the waters warmed. Even though the Elosians pumped liquibrium into Earth's waters, Emil and his sister foresaw it wouldn't be enough. Now they're working on ways to grow food from ash."

"Ash?"

"A precaution. If Etlis opens, Tarius will leave Earth in ash. Emil and Vita want to protect humans; give them a fighting chance."

A hummingbird flitted past Natalie, feasting on the nectar of a bright red blossom. Bees hummed in the lavender, while a woman scattered earthworms across the soil. Halen marveled at the beauty—at Earth's contingency plan.

"Do you want to explore a bit?" Natalie nodded toward the garden.

"No, it's better if I don't. Everything I touch ends up in rubble. No way am I screwing this place up."

"Look, if I haven't screwed it up, then no one can." Natalie smiled. "When I first arrived here, I tried to blow the whole fortress to smithereens. I even stabbed Emil with one of his own blades. And now look—he loves me."

"Yeah, well, you've been at this a lot longer than me. You have more control."

She laughed, tossing her hair back over her shoulders. "I don't have the same powers as you. Believe me, if I did, I probably would have killed us all by now."

She didn't want to tell her how messed up her magick could be—how the darkness had settled in and wouldn't accept her eviction notice. "So, the Hunters are preparing for the end?"

"Whether or not Tarius is free, our realm will need help. It's not like we haven't caused our own damage. He wants to give back to the place that has given so much to him."

"Yet not all the Hunters feel the same way." She thought of Luke and the others, how the siren population had dwindled since the Hunters built this fortress. Emil and Vita may desire peace, but their siblings wanted death.

"Aurelia likes the power of immortality. She's the kind who jumps off a building just for the thrill. Now that she has Otho, she wants to ensure she never loses him again. If the portal opens, then bye-bye. That's why *they* want our souls so badly."

"But you think we *should* let them take our souls? Do you want to just let them kill us? That kind of thinking is insane."

A gardener stopped scattering worms and glanced their way.

Natalie nudged her beneath a leafy palm, away from curious eyes. "We have to make sacrifices." She lowered her voice.

"I can take Tarius. I know it. Galadia is his weakness. You said it yourself. He wants her more than anything. If we can make him think he's getting her back—"

"Asair warned me this would happen."

"What?" What could Asair possibly warn her about? She didn't like the concerned look now taking over her sister's face.

"You're trying to be with him."

"With Tarius?" Her jaw dropped.

Natalie nodded.

"You don't know what you're saying." She studied the plants so her sister couldn't read the doubt in her eyes. She knew a part of her was searching, and even after she found Asair and Natalie, an emptiness still haunted her.

"Galadia loved him."

Halen couldn't believe Natalie would turn on her like this. "Not you too. I'm not her. I'm Halen Windspeare, very screwed up siren, who is starting to think her sister is more messed in the head than her."

"I want to fight, believe me."

"Do you?" Halen cut her off. "Because I've seen your magick. Together we could do this."

"It's more complicated than that." Natalie picked a bright bloom.

"What is it then?" Why was her sister so scared to fight? She wasn't the same girl she had faced in the hotel; the girl who released her swarm of yellow jackets on the Tari. What had changed?

Natalie glanced at her birthmark, now a dazzling metallic purple in the artificial light. "Dax wants the portal to open. You're still bound to him. Until we can get that silver out of you—"

"We're getting closer," a voice said at Halen's back.

She spun to face a slender woman, her teeth gleaming in the purple light, her dark skin glistening like diamonds.

"Jae." Halen folded into the woman's open arms. Her perfumed scent of night smoke and pepper curled beneath her nose. She sneezed.

"Sorry." Jae broke the embrace. "I've been working on a few spells."

Halen sneezed again. "It's so good to see you. Thank you for saving me from the mermaids."

"So, you admit you needed help?" Natalie's mouth turned with a smirk.

"Of course, I need help, but I need you to stop talking about giving up and spending eternity in the Hunter's arrow."

Jae hummed under her breath. "It won't come to that,

my dear ones. I'm not letting your souls near another gold arrow. I will find a way with Dax."

"Can I see him?" Dax lingered in her thoughts, never far from the seam of her soul.

"He's in my quarters. He's safe," Jae said. "It's better if there's some distance between you."

"Who would have thought we'd have to protect that doofus." Natalie cast her gaze to the lights, shaking her head. "I would love to get my hands on him."

"You stay away from that boy." Jae wagged her finger. "I don't need him jumping into your seam. He was your Guardian too, after all."

"And I'm free of him." She held up her bare arm.

"No bracelet." Jae huffed.

"I swear." Natalie crossed her heart.

Halen thought of the elixir she forced down her sister's throat back at the Tari's underground fortress. "I'm sorry about the elixir. I never should have made you drink it."

Natalie shrugged. "I didn't even feel the withdrawals with the spell Jae had me under. I was in so much pain from the arrow."

Jae touched Natalie's shoulder, her nails slender daggers capable of tearing flesh from bone, yet so gentle with her sister. "I'm sorry I couldn't have done more. I won't stop searching for a solution."

"I'm fine." Natalie removed her glasses and glanced away, wiping a tear from her cheek.

"I'm not sure I would be as positive as you," Halen said.

"I'm still processing. But we have more to worry about right now." She slid her glasses on and rolled back her shoulders. "We need to concentrate on freeing you from Dax." Natalie looked to Jae. "Nothing's working?"

"Well, since he's comatose, I've tried intravenous injections. This brought his temperature down enough to attempt extracting the silver, but every time I inject a needle in one line of the birthmark, his temperature shoots through the roof."

"You haven't hurt him yet," Halen said.

Natalie leaned forward. "You can feel his physical discomfort?"

"Everything." She pulled up her sleeve. "Even our birthmarks change together."

Jae waited for a woman in a puffy suit to pass before she spoke. "I noticed the new patterns. That's why he's so connected to your magick. It's more than the seam. It's as if you two are one."

"I don't want to be one with him. He loves the darkness. The things I've done…" Her voice trailed off as it did when death skipped through her mind.

"He loves Tarius. That could influence you as well." Jae wrapped her arm around Halen. "We will separate you two, but it isn't going to be pretty."

Halen swallowed hard. "It's going to hurt, isn't it?"

"I'm afraid so." Jae squeezed her gently.

Nothing could hurt more than the guilt for sins. She would endure Jae's methods, anything to sever the strangling Guardian bond. "Let's do it."

20

SANTA MONICA REEKED of death and decay. Asair's magick tingled along his nerves when he searched the ocean. They were out there somewhere; Rania's mutants, camouflaged in the white crests of the ocean waves, awaiting her command to surface.

Asair never dreamed Rania would bring the Krull army to the Earth realm. From Quinn's memories, he'd witnessed how the sight of land triggered Rania's fears. How she cowered beneath streetlights. She once revealed to her son that when her feet touched land, her scars burned as if she were forced to endure atonement all over again. And even though Quinn had suffered the same torture as his mother, she had abandoned him on Earth to face his demons.

Now Asair had to face his. As much as he wanted to help Halen find her siren friends, only three souls mattered to him.

"Asair. We should leave." Selene called to him from the empty boat slip.

He peered over the dock, meeting her concerned gaze. Her sisters circled the marina, feeding on fish and gulls for strength. "We'll wait." Asair knelt, lowering his voice, fearful of who might linger in the shadows.

"And if the Hunters come?" Her gaze darted between

the shore and the water. He had never seen her so unsettled. She had taken on the Krull before, torn their limbs, gnawing the leathery flesh to the bone. Her dark magick was the reason he agreed to come with her. He might despise her for what she had done to Halen, but he needed her power to take on Rania's army. He couldn't have her confidence wane now.

"Since when have you been afraid of a bunch of mutants?" He smiled, trying to calm her frantic thoughts.

She smiled back, water dripping from her black lips. "I can handle Rania's army, but it's you I'm worried about. You haven't unleashed your magick as you should. It's like you're holding back. You can't hesitate."

She had read this part of him—his fear. Never had he cast magick with such care; every action lead to a reaction, and he wouldn't ruin any more lives because of his recklessness.

"You're thinking of her again." She slipped back from the dock.

"I left with you."

"This isn't your fight. You paid the price. You lost decades in that lonely dimension. It's time to live for yourself. Let the others take care of Rania."

"You know I can't. This *is* my fight. This was always my fight. I never should have—"

"I sipped your blood willingly," she said. "I knew what it would do. Do you really think I was that naïve? I thought maybe if we were connected, you might see the way I loved you."

Selene always wanted more from him. She turned every head when she surfaced. Any mortal would have pledged their love to her. But the Guardian bond blinded him. "You know I couldn't see beyond Elizabeth. She stole my life."

"But you're free now. Don't you see? You can finally be

the siren you've always wanted to be. We can go anywhere."

"Halen wouldn't be bound to a monster if it wasn't for me. I need to do this."

"Your heart has always been so big. I don't know why you didn't have room for me." She cast her gaze to the churning water.

"I am sorry, Selene." He reached out, brushing his hand across her scaled tail, wincing inside at his creation while also marveling at the way the silver scales glistened with the glow of moonlight, in awe of darkness's captivating splendor. This wonder worried him the most. He feared Halen would discover beauty in the shadows, find the exquisite taste of dark magick, and turn away from the light as Selene had.

"We can't change the past." She swam back from his touch.

The wind whipped around them. A gust shoved the ocean water over her head, and she disappeared beneath. The boats rocked in the slips, their hulls creaking and moaning.

"Selene," he called out to her, but his voice was lost in the howling breeze.

He stood, feeling the static of magick in the air. When he turned, he spotted three figures emerging from behind one boat. His magick charged through his veins as he faced a stout boy and his companions; a girl with long silver hair, which wrapped around her muscular frame, and a slender boy with a gleaming sharp grin, young, but not from the local high school, not with those hungry eyes flashing in the night. He glanced between the boards of the dock, hoping for a little help from Selene, but found only water.

"Well, well, well. What do we have here?" the girl with the silver hair said. "Heading out for a night swim—*siren?*"

"Back away." Asair thrust his arms out, palms flat against the air. "I don't want to hurt you."

The stout boy laughed as his gaze trailed over Asair's birthmark. "You don't have a chance."

"This won't hurt as much if you don't fight." The girl crouched, placing her fingertips on the dock. As she shook her head, her cheeks sprouted with whiskers.

He stepped back. How could he kill young Etlins? They hadn't been taught the real history. They only knew the Tari lies. It wasn't their fault. "You don't want to do this."

"Actually, we do." The boy shifted, his movements mesmerizing as a plume of feathers filled his head. His skull narrowed and his nose hooked with a curved beak. As his back sprouted with wings, he leaped into the air, completing the transformation.

The girl was now a leopard, her snow-white fur bristling when she growled. She lowered her stance, nudging him farther. Asair glanced skyward as the hawk boy rushed him from behind, digging his talons into his skull. Asair cried out. With the warmth of blood on his face, his magick broke through his resistance.

He thrust his hand toward the bird. His magick crackled in the night air, illuminating the marina. The hawk cried out as Asair's blow dragged him into the water.

Selene emerged, her eyes alight with hunger.

"No!" Asair reached for the boy, but it was too late.

Selene hooked her claws into the shifter, pulling him under.

The leopard growled, running full force. She rammed Asair, shoving him into the ocean. They tumbled together, submerging in a twist of fur and claws. He untangled himself from her limbs, paddling toward the surface, and the leopard swiped him from below. His leg cut with pain, releasing the full wrath of his magick. He shoved a wave over the shifter girl's head as she clawed at the surface. Silver fins darted in the wake of his sparks, stirring the water with a dark force. He retaliated, swimming back at once.

The shifter didn't have much time before Selene claimed her, too. He cast another wave, this time to save the young shifter. He curled the water beneath her, dragging her away from Selene, forcing the water toward the shore.

Selene surfaced. Her sharp gaze met with Asair, her rage thick in the water. "Stop trying to save them all. You were made for death."

"They're innocent," he shouted over the rising winds.

"No one is innocent."

Asair had spoken the same words when he convinced her to drink his blood. He had been selfish in taking her life. He owed her, but not this way. He could never repay the debt, and perhaps she knew this, too. "We're not killing them." He shoved the shifter girl once more toward the shore.

Selene dived and thrust through the water. She snagged the shifter before she reached the sand.

The leopard girl yelped as water slipped down her throat. Kye and Diya swam to Selene's side, circling the shifter girl.

"Stop!" Asair called out.

But Selene and her sisters were deaf to his plea.

As they sliced the shifter girl, her blood spread, warming the surrounding water.

These lives were not Selene's to take.

He waved, flicking his wrist so the leopard rose over the water.

Selene jumped, clawing the leopard's paws. She hooked her fur, dragging the shifter under, swimming deep out of Asair's reach.

He pounded his fist against the water. He was tired of playing her games. Even if Selene loved him, she had an agenda. He couldn't stay with the mermaids. He had to stop what he had started so many years ago, even if it meant facing Rania on his own. Asair swam away from the safety of the dock, searching now for signs of the Krull soldiers.

Selene surfaced beside him in seconds, her scales now a shimmering black from the kill.

"Go away!" He shoved a wave in her face.

"If you don't kill them, they could come back. How do you expect to face Rania? Or should I just let the Hunters take your soul?"

He gathered the water, his magick curling the waves. "We're done." His sparks burned with his anger, seeking a release. The water warmed around them, bubbling with steam. She hated the heat, which roiled her stomach the same as rancid blood.

"What are you doing?" She fought the current now spinning with boiling water.

"What I should have done a long time ago. Maybe my soul is better off in the Hunters' arrow than with you."

When Kye surfaced, he struck her back. She howled, baring her fangs, the flesh of the leopard caught in her teeth.

He created these abominations. He could destroy them.

"You need us." Selene hissed. Her fins beat the water, but his barrier held fast.

"No, I don't!" His magick charged, shoving him up and above the steaming ocean. They stared wide-eyed while he hovered. The faces of the Elosian girls he had forced to drink his blood flashed through his mind.

Selene reached up to him, but he closed his eyes.

"I'm sorry." He released the force of his magick. The

145

waves electrified with a current of light. Screeching howls split the night air, tearing him up inside. The water splashed up around him, burning as they thrashed in the charged current. He floated higher, wishing he could escape their tortured cries. But even when the water returned to the lull of waves, he could still hear their voices ringing.

He collapsed on the dock, facing the stars with remorse and freedom tugging at his heart. No longer protected by the mermaids, he wondered if perhaps Natalie was right—maybe they were all better in the Hunters' arrows. He could make a deal with Rania. If she called off her army, then Halen would still be safe. He would surrender to the Hunters. But first, he had to make a call. He couldn't leave Halen wondering what had happened to him, not with dark magick stirring in her blood. Her rage would seek retribution.

He closed his eyes, exhaling slowly to steady the sparks. He no longer needed marrow from

Elizabeth to recover, but a little rest before he called Halen would ensure his magick wouldn't waver. As he inhaled, the wind whipped alongside the docks. A scurried rush brushed his ears, followed by a broken howl. He opened his eyes to find a snarling Krull commander, sickle in hand, at the end of the dock; its eyes, long slits in the warrior's mammoth skull, glowed with anticipation. Below the creature's waist, spiked, steel-gray quills quivered, set for battle.

Asair's veins burned. His gaze darted to the water, hoping for an escape when he spotted the grotesque mutant army charging the shore. Their beady yellow eyes illuminated the path. In the center of the battalion, a woman emerged. Her angered energy swirled around her like a torrid storm searching for her next target to decimate. When her sharp gaze met with Asair, memories of

Quinn's mother rushed him all at once. His magick sparked, then faded as quickly as Quinn's love and hatred for this mother fought his urge to strike.

If Rania had any feelings left for her son, it didn't show, for she let out a series of whooping calls, releasing her army onto the beach.

Asair reached out, wiggling his fingertips, searching for any spark to rise.

She waved, commanding the Krull soldier before him.

Focused on his lack of magick, he didn't even see the dagger poised in the air before the blade plunged into this back.

Rania screamed from the shore. "No, you fool. Not that one."

Asair's fingers brushed the hilt, but he could not reach far enough to yank it out. He hurled as the pain seared through to his bones, his blood catching on fire. As he turned, he caught a flicker of gold. He wanted to scream out to the Krull who had stabbed him, warn him to turn, but the flames and vomit stole his voice.

A Hunter bent over the Krull warrior, striking the beast across the jaw. Ezra's face broke with a smile as he reached over his shoulder for his gold arrow. Perhaps if the Hunter was still the siren boy Halen had adored, Asair would have a chance, but with Otho's soul in control, and his magick on hiatus, he didn't see a way out. Avoiding the glimmer of gold, he cast his gaze to the heavens, breathing in the sweet, salty air, centering all thoughts now on the girl who would never forgive him for dying.

21

"WE HAVEN'T HEARD BACK from Vita. I'm worried." Halen rubbed her arm, now stained a purplish black hue from Jae's potion, but still, the annoying sliver shone through. No matter what herb or incantation Jae cast, the fused silver wouldn't budge. Halen was determined it would work, though. She would endure the pain if it freed her from Dax. They had to try harder, work faster, so she could leave to join the fight.

"Emil's making calls now. He's spoken to Tasar, but there's no sign of the Hunters, Rania, or even the mermaids."

"Tasar?" As Halen rose to a sitting position, her head swam. The tiny glass potion vials on Jae's counter all blended into a rainbow blur.

Jae rushed over, lowering her back to the pillows. "You need to rest. This is hard when you're still healing from the mermaid venom. I can't have you bleeding to death like —" She averted her gaze.

"You can say her name—Tage," Halen said. "Tage was tough. She would have been right here by my side trying to help." Speaking her name tugged at her heart. She missed her friend, but she had to fight because of her—for all the sirens who risked their lives, so her heart stayed beating. If she didn't fight, they lost their lives for nothing.

"I'm sure she would." Jae exhaled a slow breath. "But I don't want to push you anymore."

"I'm fine." Halen reached for her. "Just give Dax the next dose. The sooner I'm free of him, the sooner I'll heal."

Jae's gaze slipped to Natalie.

"I can take it," Halen assured her sister. Natalie hadn't left her side, holding her hand when the fever boiled, absorbing her sparks when they threatened to strike Jae's spell. Though they hadn't grown up together, already Natalie felt like family. She had the same caring nature as their mother. It comforted Halen just having her by her side. If it were the other way around, she would do the same for her sister.

Natalie nodded. "Give it to Dax. I'll take care of her."

Halen managed a faint smile. The last dose tore through her like fire ants charging through her veins. Dax, however, looked much worse. His arm welted with bubbled wounds, his blond hair had turned a violet gray, and his skin beaded with sweat. Halen prayed the next dose penetrated the silver. If Jae could just hit the melting point without killing them both, then she might be able to extract the remnants of the bracelet.

Her assistant, a bird-like girl with a hooked nose and a plume of bright pink hair, stood by Jae, ready with a long needle. When Jae whispered an incantation, the girl punctured Dax's arm.

Halen's skin pricked; she winced, anticipating the excruciating pain sure to follow. She pinched her eyes shut as the scent of burning charcoal filled the air.

Jae chanted and with each syllable, the pain intensified with a throbbing, pulsing pressure. Halen grasped Natalie's hand. Her arms shook, the vibration of Jae's spell rolling across her chest, and she jerked wildly as spasms of dagger-sharp sparks jolted through her.

"This is too much!" Natalie shouted.

Halen forced words to her throat. "Don't... stop."

"The silver's melting." Jae's assistant pulled the needle up ever so slightly, and the tube filled with a shiny liquid.

"Hang in there." Natalie ran a damp cloth over her forehead, patting away the sweat with her free hand.

Halen's eyes rolled in the back of her head; her jaw clenched as the fire spread. She could do this. She had to do this. If only...

"Stop!" Dax's warbled cry cut the air. He thrust his arm out, and the girl flew back, hitting the wall. She jumped up, securing his flaying arm with bands.

The monitors beeped with their spiking heartbeats.

"The spell's working!" Natalie shouted.

With this hope, Halen fought the next surge as Jae injected the needle into her arm.

Jae continued her chant, her tone deepening with each syllable.

Halen writhed with the heat inside her, growing hotter and hotter. Her sparks surged, answering the call to protect her, and she tried to push them back. But she couldn't contain the storm inside her. Her head tilted back, her eyes opened wide, unleashing a bright light.

The light bounced across the room, sending books and scrolls, vials and brass bowls crashing to the ground. Natalie's wheelchair flew back, ramming the shelves. She toppled sideways and onto the floor.

Jae reached for the needle, but another surge of light shot her back, throwing her up into the air. Jae's body jerked, her skin transforming with dragon scales. Her eyes bulged as horns sprouted from her head. "I can't fight the transformation!"

"We're losing him." Her assistant fought the shaking needle. "We have to stop."

The monitor beeped, squealing with the high-pitched alarm of death, then fell silent.

Jae collapsed back to the ground. She righted herself at once. Shaking her head and rolling her neck, her bones cracked as her wings sprouted from her back. "Extract the silver!" Jae's voice came out as a growl. "This is our only chance."

"Halen's magick is too powerful. It's forcing me away. She's protecting the Guardian." The girl's needle wavered over his arm while her gaze darted between the silent monitor and Halen. "She'll kill us all!"

With a wave of her hand, Natalie righted her chair and wheeled beside the girl. "Go! Get out of here." She grasped the needle. "I've got this."

"You should have let Emil take her." The girl rushed from the room.

Curved black claws sprouted from Jae's feet, yet her voice remained steady; her words of magick spun Halen's thoughts.

"Hang in there!" Natalie shouted.

Halen grasped the pillows, clutching them to her chest as the fire spread. Another flash shot from her eyes. This time, in the bright light, Halen caught the glimmer of charred antlers. Her breath rushed in and out of her chest as smoke choked the air.

"Help her." Natalie sounded so far away.

Jae's face blurred in and out of her vision—half woman, half-dragon

"*Plomo kryrptolo!*" Jae shouted.

Smoke filled Halen's lungs—breath, an unattainable wish.

"Halen!" Jae slapped her face, her dragon claws catching the flesh of her cheek. "Wake up!"

Follow me. A whispered voice rushed through her thoughts.

A white butterfly floated before her, its delicate wings singing. The insect floated up and away, heading toward a cool breeze. She ran after the butterfly, following it across the bridge, over the crimson river, and down the ash-coated bank. With each step, the pain lessened, and Jae's voice grew fainter. A part of her wanted to stop, but compelled by the butterfly, she found she could not turn back.

She ran farther, her pace steady as she trudged through the ash until Jae's voice was no more than a whisper. When the butterfly drifted into the burning forest, her heart flooded with fear. "Don't go!" she called to the butterfly.

The insect fluttered into the flames.

She darted to save the creature, but a magnificent stag headed her off. The beast stood before her, its fur stained in soot, its gold-coated antlers gleaming against the flames. She gasped as she met the creature's black stare and saw the butterfly perched in the crook of its grand antlers.

Halen stumbled, backing away as the stag edged closer. She had seen this creature before in the forest, the day she had left Asair—the day she had sealed the portal with her soul. Etlis could only open one way... She touched her chest, her heart beating with life beneath her fingertips. Her gaze darted to the swirling red sky above, where dragons howled with tortured cries.

The sweltering winds swept the ash at her feet in a spiral of decay. She closed her eyes, holding her breath, and finally, when the ash settled, she dared to peek.

A young man stood before her. His skin curled from the bone along his jawline, the tendons in his neck a raw red. His eyebrows were singed, and his dark hair fell in patches across his burned skull. He wore pants of shimmering dragon scales, his muscled chest bare. Pinned to the lapel of his fur vest, the butterfly struggled for freedom. He held his hand out to her. "Welcome home."

As the thick smoke choked Halen's breath, Tarius' *welcome* stole the last from her lungs. With a glance at his offered hand, her courage roiled inside. If she was in Etlis, then Jae's spell had failed. But why, then, did she feel the heat of the realm pressing against her flesh? Why did her pulse surge when she met Tarius' haunting gaze? If she was dead, she shouldn't feel anything at all.

Driven by the fear coursing through her veins, she bolted, heading straight into the burning forest. The thunderous pounding of hooves against the ruins of Etlis chased her deeper into the crackling flames. Hopping over a burning log, her toe caught in the fire. She pounded her foot in the ash as the stag leaped over the burning brush. She bolted, now ducking beneath the black, curled branches. Halen dared not glance over her shoulder with the stag steady at her heels. She coughed the tickle in her throat away, but soon her lungs absorbed the dense air, and she buckled as the smoke stole her gait.

A breeze fell at the back of her neck. She turned into the stag's muzzle.

It's not so bad. You'll get used to the heat. His voice entered her thoughts.

Halen shook her head, unable to find words, unable to fathom a night in this burning hell with this monster. She side-stepped the beast and darted across the field. Though the ground scorched beneath her feet, she forced each step, begging that her legs wouldn't give out.

Ahead, a stone tower emerged from the smoke. A part of her sang with a warning that this too was a trap, but with her focus set on the curved entrance, she sprinted. When she dashed inside, the clattering clomps of hooves silenced.

Clasping the stone railing, she strode up the winding staircase, listening for the stag, peering out each tower window as she ascended, checking to see if he was watching from below. With no direction in mind but away from Tarius, she took the stairs two at a time, climbing for what felt like hours. Her muscles burned in her calves, her lungs ached for breath, and her legs wobbled, threatening to collapse, but she wouldn't allow him to reach her.

She tripped over the last step, stumbling into a circular room. She froze, fear skipping along her shattered nerves. The only escape from the stone tower was an open window far above Etlis.

She scanned the room. A stone altar sat in the center, a tall mirror, swiped clean except for the sooty fingerprints, propped against one wall, and beside the mirror was a glass birdcage, which hung by an ornate metal hook from the domed ceiling.

Between choked breaths, she folded, clutching her stomach. Her eyes widened as her gaze landed at her feet. She wriggled her toes, the nails black, the skin of her little toe burnt to the bone. Brushing away the ash, she reached for her foot, when the coughing consumed her. Stumbling, she grasped the altar, knocking into the mirror. When she turned, she screamed.

And the monstrous girl reflected, mimicked her cry.

22

HER THROAT BURNED as she screamed at her gruesome reflection. "No, no, no!" Halen touched her cheek, her fingers finding a bone. Her hair clumped at her scalp, strands of gray and violet curled over her flesh-torn shoulder. She leaned closer to the mirror, wiping away the soot, not believing it was her. Skin peeled back from her jawline, the mandible charred. She worked her jaw from side to side and her lips cracked crimson. Parched, she licked away the blood.

Halen fanned her skirt, the lace dress frayed like her flesh. As she ran her hand over the silk ribbon, she spotted a feather poking from her wrist bone. Her eyes widened. Dusty black feathers coated her wrist up to the crook of her elbow. She touched the sharp tip with her finger. She tugged the feather harder. When she twisted it free, her skin stung as if she'd been pinched.

"I apologize for your new body," a voice said at her back.

Reflected in the mirror was Tarius, standing in the doorway, blocking the stairway. His energy consumed the room, calling to her fear.

"Finding a host in Etlis is difficult. I knew one day you would come. I kept her for you. She's the last of her generation." He nodded toward the open birdcage. "We will cross soon enough. Maybe you can even take your old body back if you like?"

Halen held her hand up, cringing at her charred finger-tips, wondering if they might fall off from the simple action. Though her appearance frightened her, her companion terrified her more. "Tarius," she said.

He smiled, closing his eyes, breathing in her voice. "To hear my name from your lips. Well, not quite your lips, but the sound comes from your soul." He pounded his chest.

This was the monster responsible for all the death—for her mother's. Her anger swelled in her stomach and the emotion made her falter. She wouldn't be able to fight him in this condition. Her gaze darted to the window, the desire to jump growing favorable. "How did I get here—inside Etlis?"

"Your heart stopped beating. I will reward Dax. He served the Tari best of all. He's a wonderful Guardian." His dark gaze landed on her. "Galadia. You don't know how long I've waited." He stepped toward her, his bare feet black with ash.

"My name is Halen." She edged away.

"In your last life, yes. But it was so short, you will easily forget in time and claim your true self."

She wouldn't listen. She was Halen Windspeare, daughter of Corinne, sister to Natalie. Other than not having her body, she was exactly who she should be. The force of her magick could crumble this tower. She had faced demons, mermaids, and monsters. But not in this fragile body.

He licked his lips, and she cringed inside. He rolled his broad shoulders back, bearing his chiseled chest where the skin peeled back, revealing exposed muscle.

She would need magick to fight him off, but though he inched closer, her sparks didn't rise. "Am I dead?"

"Quite, but for us to leave, one more must die."

Her mind raced with thoughts of her sister and Asair. Had she hurt Natalie when they had tried to extract the silver? Was Natalie… No. She shook the thought away. She wouldn't allow him to get in her head.

He crossed the room and stood at the window. "It won't take long. Plans are in place."

"Natalie and Asair won't fall for your tricks."

A sly smile filled his face. "You don't know? Well, of course not. You've been so busy trying to die that you didn't get the news."

"What news?" She hugged her new body, her fingers sliding against a rib bone.

"He's already dead."

"What are you talking about? Who?" Her thoughts grew frantic.

He drew a breath and blew. The smoke curled, forming letters before her eyes.

A S A I R

The smoky letters blurred with her tears. "Liar!" She beat the air, sweeping his name away. Asair had the mermaids by his side. His magick was strong. He couldn't be dead; she would feel it. "You're a liar!"

"How else do you think you arrived here? I wouldn't have been able to reach you unless…"

"Stop! I don't want to hear anymore." She covered her ears, turning away. She wouldn't let this monster speak of Asair. He wasn't dead. This she knew for sure. He wouldn't leave her, only to die.

Tarius touched her arm, and she struck out, clipping his cheek. His skin caught in her nails, ripping from his face. She screamed. "What the hell?" She swiped his skin off on her skirt.

"This isn't hell." He glanced in the mirror and patted his cheek, peeling off the hanging bits of flesh. "But if you keep that up, we'll look quite hellish."

"I think we're past that point." She held up her arm; the skin was broken with feathers poking through.

He laughed. "Oh, you're quite right." He ripped the remaining skin from the side of his face. "What's the use in trying. We'll have new bodies soon enough. When Dax kills your sister, he will free us both."

"Natalie can handle Dax." As Tarius patted his face where she tore the skin, she thought maybe she could obliterate him. Still, she hesitated.

He shook his head, humming under his breath. "Dax is a Guardian to you both."

"She's free of him. Natalie can cast magick without Dax."

He chuckled. "Of course she can. Any blue moon siren can learn to cast magick without the elixir, but that doesn't prevent him from entering her seam."

"I haven't released him. He can't touch her."

He leaned against the wall, crossing his arms. "You're here, aren't you? Death proceeds any formalities."

She loathed his cocky stare. With his body so mangled, she wondered how hard it would be to pop his eyes right out of their sockets. "You don't know how the Guardian bond works."

"I created it." He smiled. "And I'm pretty sure Dax can control your sister's magick now."

Was this true or another attempt at shaking her confidence? But Dax had said he could only be Guardian to one, and she hadn't released him yet. "Dax led me here. I followed the white butterfly in Etlis. We're still connected."

"Dax sent the butterfly?" His charred eyebrows rose. "Interesting."

"Why do you care?" She didn't like the look on his face. He seemed almost pleased.

"We should hurry if you want to return to your body."

"I'm not leaving with you." She had made this mistake

in Asair's dimension, taking the demon with her instead of killing him. This time only one would leave Etlis or no one at all.

"If your body is of no use to you, then we can take our time. But I'm sure Dax won't be long with your sister."

"You underestimate Natalie."

"And you underestimate the Guardian bond." He smiled. "All that beautiful power of yours will never be free." He raised his fist in her face. "I will always have a grip on you. You will never leave me again. You and I will renew our vows."

Her breath quickened. "Vows?" What didn't he get about this? She wasn't playing games. "I would rather die!"

He chuckled. "Halen Windspeare is already dead. When we have the water stone, your soul will remember— you will be Galadia once more. Etlis will be ours. Her powers—your powers—can bring back life." He waved out the window. "You have the gift to restore this realm."

She joined him by the open window. A vast realm glowed with flames below. Dragons beat the sky, their tortured cries echoing in the air with wings on fire, mimicking the call of her loss and despair.

"Their magick keeps them alive, though they're burning inside and out. You'll get used to the sound," Tarius said.

"I could never." Halen hugged herself, her body so frail as if it might transform to dust with her next breath. She had bent to the will of Dax. She had followed everyone's plans so willingly, but she wasn't the same girl. Her sister's soul would live; Emil would make sure of it. If she had to stay in the flames to protect Earth and Elosia, she would. But not by this monster's side.

With the desire to leap from the window, her body stirred with a strange sort of tickling feeling. The feathers on her wrist poked through her skin, elongating. She shook her hand and her arm shifted to a wing. She marveled at the fine feathers untouched by flames.

"That's not a good idea." Tarius's tone held warning. "The body inside is undamaged by the wreckage of Etlis. I'm afraid it might be all that's keeping you together."

Halen shook, remembering Lina's actions back in the forest that day. She wriggled until her feet vanished and her legs tucked up under her belly, and she fluttered up into the air. She darted out the window, flying across the barren land, her tattered wings beating the thick smoke. The river flowed crimson, bones of the dead lining the banks; the beauty of Etlis swallowed in Tarius's rage.

A dragon's wings churned the air above. When she glanced skyward, the dragon spread its jaws. She beat her little wings faster. The dragon swooped beside her, brushing her body with its horn. The motion threw her flight off balance, sending her spiraling toward a bank of bones. With her wings tucked at her sides, she cried for salvation as the ground neared where the empty sockets of a skull stared up, welcoming her death.

"No!" The word came out of her beak as a screeching squawk. And as her will to live ignited, her wings spread out by her sides. Her body drifted, slowing her descent.

Again, the tickling rustled her feathers, and as she touched the ash ground, her body transformed. Her toes sunk in the ash, the soles of her feet burning, but as much as she fought the transformation, she stood as the fragile girl once more.

Shadows of wings darkened the ground as the beasts hovered. She scanned the landscape for a hiding place. Beyond the crimson river, the mouth of a forest of rocks called to her. The granite spires spiked the sky, reaching toward the three crescent moons. She darted toward the shelter, slipping through the entrance.

When her arm touched the rock walls, her skin sizzled.

She screamed, clutching her elbow. She pressed her arms in front of her, trying to make herself as small as possible. Should she shift? She thought her bird form might navigate the maze of rocks better, but she also didn't feel comfortable as a bird. It seemed only instinct guided her actions when in the bird form, and right now she needed reason.

The beasts cried out, furious at the rock tips barring them from entering. Still, the dragons darted back and forth, searching for a way to her. Despite her feeble legs, she ran. Her skin split along her thigh with the movement. Panicked, she might fall apart, and her carcass left to burn, a surge of sparks tickled her skin. Not the same as when she transformed, but the familiar sparks of magick.

A dragon whipped its tail against the spires, knocking them one by one, so they crumbled behind her, blocking her from turning back. Dagger sharp fragments rained in heavy waves, and she picked up her pace to keep from being crushed. She came to a clearing, a trap, and the dragons circled, waiting for her to enter.

She searched for another place to hide, but she would have to cross the open space to get to the next outcrop. Her fear spun her sparks, charging across her chest, wrapping her beating heart. The magick might tear her apart, but she wouldn't survive if she ran.

Halen waved, and the ash swept upward with her command. The ash spiraled, swarming the dragon, and forcing the beast away. Two more dragons swooped in, taking its place. She waved again, but this time her magick fizzled. She shook her hands, but her magick would not rise.

Halen glanced back at the barricade behind her and then to the opposite side, where a stag stood waiting. She resisted the urge to call out his name, to plead for help, but already he charged toward her. As the dragon swooped down, the stag scooped her with his antlers, thrusting her over and onto his back. She clutched his fur, tucking her chest against his neck.

Sparks ran through her, reaching deep within her soul. Like lightning on a dark summer night, the boy's face emerged. He smiled, and despite the smoke, his breath, sweet like honey, filled her mouth. She rolled her tongue against the roof of her mouth, fighting the memories of his kisses. His heartbeat thrummed in her ears, calling her back to him. She cried into the fur, screaming her frustration. "I hate you!" She pounded her fist against the stag.

He bounded into the forest of charred trees. The dragons loom overhead, swaying in the breeze, but they rescinded their attack when the stag cast his gaze skyward. She wasn't the only one frightened of him.

He knocked her off carefully, and she tumbled into the soft ash.

Striking his hoof on the ground, the transformation was effortless; the young man stood before her once more. He offered his hand.

"Get away from me." She scooted back, wishing she could bury under the ash and away from his piercing gaze.

"I've waited too long to have you become a dragon's dinner."

"I don't love you." Though feeling his pulse against hers, she knew full well Galadia had. Somehow, she loved this monster, but her soul also knew there was a reason she had left—a reason driven by fear.

As if reading her thoughts, Tarius spoke. "You're not thinking of leaving—are you?"

She averted her gaze to the ground, terrified a part of her soul wanted to stay.

"You will remember how good it feels to love me."

She shook her head, her body trembling. "No, I won't."

"I should have never let you go. I should have fought

harder. But what I can't understand is why you never came back to me. I waited by the shore every full moon until—"

"Stop!" Halen held up her hand. "I'm not her. I know you've been here a long time and spent a bazillion years thinking of her and what happened, but Galadia's dead. Let it go. Whatever happened between the two of you isn't going to happen again."

"Did you touch the stone?"

She swallowed hard. The desert of death flashed through her thoughts. She glanced away.

"You did." He chuckled. "Then you know full well what you're capable of. Is that why she never returned? Did Galadia cave to the calling of the stone?" He laughed once more, letting out a whooping holler. "All these years I thought she had found another love, but she succumbed to the darkness—didn't she? Galadia had an undying thirst for blood. It's what I loved most about her."

"You're wrong." Halen shook her head. "Galadia was the mother of Elosia. The realm is beautiful."

"Of course, it's beautiful. She had exceptional taste. Especially when it came to death."

Halen wouldn't listen to his lies. She had seen Jae's book about the history of Elosia. How the heavens gave Tarius the fire stone to build Etlis, and Galadia the water stone for Elosia. Elosia, with its azure rivers, indigo sky, and rainbow dusted caverns was the most stunning place she had ever seen. A demon's heart couldn't fathom Elosia. He was trying to get into her head. Yet, she couldn't deny the urge winding through her magick that night in the desert, something calling beyond the Guardian bond. The same wanton call for blood still begged for a release.

Love and death spoke to her soul. Like his honeyed kisses, she craved the thrill death brought her. Given the chance, she would kill them all again.

23

Inhaling a deep breath, the heavy stench of gasoline and rubber filled Asair's lungs. He rolled to his side, clutching his ribs. Staring down at him from the hood of a beat-up Charger sat Vita, scrolling through her cell phone. He grasped his chest, his fingers fumbling over his shirt buttons, finally resting on a gauzy strip of bandage soaked through with blood. Otho's determined stare flashed through his mind. If the gold arrow had punctured him, how was he still alive? "What happened?"

She hopped off the car. "Your heart stopped for a few minutes. I had to perform CPR."

"And I did a little magick to stop the bleeding." A waif of a girl stepped from the shadows. Behind her towered a boy with curly auburn hair.

Asair smiled. "Thank you, Lina."

"I carried your sorry ass here." Tasar grinned. "Who would have thought I'd have to rescue the powerful Asair."

"I'm forever grateful." Asair nodded.

"We've all been catering to you for the last three hours." Vita peered out the window, then turned back to him. "Get up. We have to go—now."

Vita had never been one with words, but he needed answers. "It wasn't a gold arrow?"

"No, not gold. I deflected Otho's arrow," Lina said.

"My sister Aurelia stabbed you with her dagger. Not to mention you had a Krull blade in your back." Vita frowned.

"Knife wounds. That's why I feel this way." He took in the service garage, the only light cast from a flashing neon sign. A car sat above on a hoist, with scattered tools beneath. He rose to a sitting position, wincing as his bandage tugged his wound. "Where are we?"

"A shifter owns this garage." Tasar rummaged through the tool chest. "She's fine, but she won't want us to stay much longer. She doesn't want any trouble." "And Rania?" Asair hoped she had retreated.

"She's a coward. She bolted below the waves when the fire rings crisped the coastline." Vita rolled her eyes.

"The portal thinned when my heart stopped, didn't it?"

Lina nodded. "The damage is extensive."

"Damn it. I shouldn't have been so careless." He grabbed the workbench, using it to stand.

Vita rushed to help him to his feet, hooking her arm through his. "Let's just say the portal wavered, but at least it sent Rania and her army back underwater. My brothers and sister will look for us, though. We need to get back to the fortress."

The one thing he knew for certain from Quinn's memories was that a little fire wouldn't scare Rania. She would return. His head throbbed more.

Vita's cell phone rang. She took it out of her pocket, glancing at the screen. "It's Natalie." She tucked the phone back in her jacket.

"Answer it." He squeezed her arm.

"We need to get out of here first." She nodded toward the old car. "The Charger's gutted. No engine." She propped him against the wall, then opened the garage doors and peered into the yard where three more cars sat parked. "Hopefully, one of those starts." She grabbed all the keys from the hooks and hit the fobs until one beeped. "Let's go." She wrapped her arm around his waist and he fumbled.

"I've got him." Tasar took her place.

His grip was firm at Asair's side, but for such a burly young man, he was careful not to agitate his wounds. "Thank you." Asair nodded as they headed into the yard.

"Don't thank me yet. We still have to get you back to the fortress."

Lina rushed ahead, keeping a keen eye on the shadows. Vita hopped in the driver's seat and Tasar guided Asair to the seat beside him.

Vita's cell phone rang again as she started the car. She tossed the phone to Asair. He caught it, though the quick movement burned along his shoulder blade.

Tasar and Lina jumped into the back seat.

Vita veered the car into the empty street, revving the engine.

"Slow down. You're going to draw attention." He placed his hand on her knee.

She shot him a pointed stare, and he withdrew his hand at once. The phone buzzed, and he answered, hopeful to hear the one voice he longed for. He needed to apologize to Halen. Let her know he had made a terrible mistake and he would never leave again. "Hello."

"Asair?" Natalie's voice cracked. "You're alive!"

"I'm fine. I'm with Vita, Tasar, and Lina. I'll put you on speaker." He held the phone so they all could hear her.

"I thought you were dead." She sniffed.

Was she crying? "Why now, darling, don't you have any faith in me?"

"What the hell happened?" She sniffed again.

"My heart stopped for a few seconds. That's all. We're heading back now."

They passed a coffee shop, the spinning doughnut sign

in flames. Firefighters lined the street with hoses. Alarms wailed along the coastline as waves beat the shore, but his focus stayed with the girl now sobbing on the other end of the line. His insides rolled with fear. "Natalie, what's the matter?"

"Tarius…" Her voice was so small, reminding him of when she woke after Jae's magick and realized for the first time she couldn't walk. This same uncertainty plagued her voice now.

"Natalie, tell me what's happened."

"We tried to get the silver out—separate Dax from Halen. It was going so well, but I guess when your heart stopped beating—" There was a long, breathless pause.

"What are you saying?" Vita spoke for him.

"Halen's dead."

His chest caved. What was this madness? She couldn't be dead. He had left her in the safest place. He had left to protect her. The car rumbled, shaking with his grief.

Vita shot him a warning glance as she fought to keep the car on the road.

"What happened?" Lina leaned forward, clutching the seat.

"Tarius took her soul," Natalie whispered. "Halen's in Etlis."

As the weight of her words hit them head on, Vita slammed her foot to the accelerator. She sped through the red light, not looking back as she swerved onto the highway. The city lights bled into one another as Asair's emotions spun.

"Jae thinks we have about eleven hours to get her soul back in her body before her magick completely diminishes. But if Tarius makes her say his vows, then she's lost to us forever."

"We're heading to the airport," Vita said. "Ask Emil to call ahead—have the pilot prepare a plane." "That will

167

take too long. Help is already on the way. Where are you?"

"We're on the highway now." Vita leaned forward, searching for a sign. "Track the phone."

"We're tracking your scent."

A heavy thud pounded the roof of the car. Asair raised his hand to strike with magick as the car lifted into the air.

Vita grasped his wrist. "Don't!"

Talons ripped through the roof, piercing the metal. "Jae's got us now. Let Emil know we're on our way." Vita nodded to Lina, and she ended the call.

Asair pressed the button, lowering the car window, and peered out. Jae's wings beat the night air, and the flaming city below was a reminder of the girl trapped in a burning realm. He punched the dash, screaming out his anger. Below, windows burst from house frames, sidewalks split, and car alarms wailed with the echo of his tortured cry.

I'M RIGHT HERE.

Halen rolled to her side. Asair stood by her bed. Heavy soot streaked his shirt and his pants were frayed from outrunning Etlis's relentless flames.

I knew you'd come back. Get me out of here. She reached for his hand.

You're not coming with me.

In his fist, she caught the glint of a dagger.

What the hell?

He stepped toward her; his gaze unwavering as he lifted the blade.

Asair, stop!

He swung the dagger downward and with a swooping jab, he plunged the blade deep into her chest.

Fiery pain seared through her body. The betrayal crushed her breath. She grasped the hilt as the blood oozed from the wound; her gaze never leaving his. *Why?* Her words were but a whisper. She jolted awake, clutching her heaving chest.

Tarius sat at her side, his weathered feet propped up on the stone altar.

"Bad dreams?" When he cocked his head, the few remaining locks of hair he had left fell to the side, revealing an open hole where his ear should be.

"How did I get here?" His presence repulsed her, and she couldn't get his words out of her mind:

Galadia had an undying thirst for blood. It's what I loved the most about her. She sat with the flats of her hands on the altar, the stone warm against her palms.

"You passed out. A siren soul in a shifter body will take time to adjust, and I assume your sister is trying to bring you back."

"I will go back." She had to go back. At least she hoped there was a way.

"At what cost? Do you know what your death and Asair's death have done to Earth?"

"The spell is bound in three."

He shrugged. "And two of you are dead."

As much as she wanted to slap him once more for reminding her, she shoved her grief aside. She wouldn't allow Asair's death to take root. "You said I still had time to get my body back, which means I'm not fully dead."

He glanced away.

"I'm not dead," she said. "Am I?"

"Even if you reconnect with your body, unless you embrace your past life, you won't be able to save Etlis. The powers of the water stone belong to Galadia. Unless…." He peeked up, meeting her gaze. "You give it to me."

"You can't touch it."

"There is a way." His mouth lifted with a sickening grin.

As she bit back her lip, a tooth popped out. She slapped her hand over her mouth, watching the tooth roll along the floor.

"I could always keep you safe in there." He nodded to the glass cage.

"Absolutely not." She shuddered. No way would she be his prisoner. She would never be anyone's prisoner again, but she had to find a way out and quickly before her shifter body disintegrated. "Why do you want the stone?" She shifted away from the subject of her incarceration.

"Darkness is the only way they will see."

"Who?"

"Humans, shifters, Elosians, they always search for more, striving so hard for validation, when they are born superb." He sighed. "They don't believe in their given power. They doubt themselves and try to become someone else, turning away from who they were born to be."

"How will dark magick help them?" Halen didn't like where this conversation was heading. She had succumbed to the dark sparks, embraced, a part of herself she had denied; a part of her she had been told was bad—dangerous. But at that moment, she had never felt more alive.

"Darkness is the balance to the light. The realms have been in the light too long, and all they see are their flaws. Darkness will allow them to reunite with their power without shame or judgment."

She huffed, glancing out the window. Her thoughts spun with the pleasure of killing; the sight of blood called to the dark magick, but the guilt of taking another's life always tugged her back. If she answered the call of evil, she feared she may never return. "You think everyone wants to die in flames?"

"No, everyone just wants to stop trying so hard to be something they are not. No one needs to hide in the shadows of their true self if darkness reigns."

"That's the most warped theory. Do you know how wrong that is?"

"Then consider the alternative." His face contorted with a twisted smirk, which reached his gleaming eyes. "I will allow your sister to live if you say the vows."

"We are not negotiating."

"Saying the vows is the only way to save Etlis. The fires will cease, and your shifter friends can return home. That

171

is what you want—isn't it? To save the world." His tone held a mocking ring to it.

"I will stop the fires," she said.

"Then you'll renew your vows to me and stay." He nodded.

"I didn't say that." She scooted away from him. She thought she had been quite clear about her intentions. "Conflict doesn't need to exist. If you just love me…" Pain flecked his eyes—an open wound that had bled for over a hundred years. "Why is that so hard for you? Is it because of this body? Do wish for the old me?"

"I could never love you." She shoveled salt into his emotional wound.

He stood with his fists clenched by his sides. "When you shed this Halen Windspeare girl, then your soul will see. Come." He dragged her from the altar and across the room. For such a frail body, his strength was overwhelming. He shoved her against the frame of the open window. "Do you want Earth to suffer this fate?"

"We are stronger than you think." She shoved away from him. "Not everyone is hiding from their power. And once they see what they are fighting for, then you won't have a chance."

"You put too much faith in your kind. Already, they are exhausted. They crave darkness—the realms will welcome me."

She thought of the Hunters' garden; life sprouting out of ashes. The Hunters prepared, but first death would come. Millions would die because she couldn't love this demon. Did she have faith in humans? She had traveled to the dark parts of her seam; the temptation was so easy to accept. Earth didn't need an extra shove toward the darkness—they needed a fighting chance.

"Just accept me. Renew Galadia's vows and bring back

the wand. As long as you are by my side, I will never use my magick against Earth. Your sister will live."

She turned, facing him, loathing every inch of his rotting flesh and dark soul, yet the mention of the water stone piqued her interest. It wasn't in Etlis, so *she* would have to leave to retrieve Galadia's wand. Did he have a way out?

Her thoughts spun, working through each scenario. If she could get to her sister, together they had the strength to destroy him. If she at least said the vows, then it would appease him. It would give her the time she needed. Halen had to take the chance that Galadia never returned to him because she had stopped loving this monster. She had to believe her heart would never want him again. She would say the words Tarius wanted to hear, knowing Halen Windspeare's heart would never bend to his will.

IN ALL HIS YEARS, even trapped in a dimension, Asair had never felt more out of control. His magick rolled beneath his skin, seeking a release, but he had no direction to cast his sparks until he could face the demon who took Halen. "Where is she?" Asair brushed past Natalie, bumping into her wheelchair.

"Slow down." She grasped his hand and withdrew at once. "You need to control that." She shook her hand. "You can't see her right now—not when your magick's so erratic."

"I have to." He didn't have time to argue with her. "She's part of me—she's part of you." He pounded his chest.

"I understand, but you can't help her now." Natalie bowed her head.

"I just want to see her." He slowed his breath, calming the force traveling through his veins. He knelt before Natalie and placed his hands on her knees. She didn't flinch back. "See, I can control it."

"For a minute." She crossed her arms.

He met her gaze. "Please."

"She's in Jae's quarters. But you need to know something..."

He hopped up. "I'll be fine once I see her." He called

over his shoulder, taking off down the hall. He quickened his pace to a sprint, his magick surging with each step. After holding his magick back and then letting loose at the ocean, the air charged around him, his senses livened. He tasted the smoke of Jae's quarters on his tongue before he even reached the door. But what he didn't expect when he passed the next room was to find Dax sitting on the leather sofa, sipping tea from a china cup.

The magick he'd tamed only moments before now electrified in his cells.

Jae stepped from the room, blocking his view of Dax. She placed her hand over his racing heart.

"He's awake?" He glanced up at her.

"There were complications." She inhaled a deep breath and exhaled. "But we can fix this. I can bring Halen back."

"What is *he* doing here?" He peered around the towering woman.

Dax's hand shook as he set the teacup on the saucer. The Guardian birthmark glittered in the dim light; bruises blotched his arm, and silver flecked his clothes.

"Did you get that poison out of her?" Asair asked. "Is she free of him?"

"We can't remove the silver." Her tone was firm as if holding a warning.

But he didn't heed it. Asair pushed past Jae, using the force of magick to throw her off balance. "Dax doesn't need to live. He doesn't deserve to breathe." He thrust his hand outward, and the sofa burst with flames.

Dax leaped to his feet. "Asair!" His voice came out as a growl. "I'm still bound to her."

"And I will unbind you." He needed to feel his pulse wane in his grip. He rushed Dax, shoving him to the ground.

"Get off me!" Dax rolled, punching out.

"Let him go." Jae was at his back, but he spun the curtains around her, yanking her back and binding her in the velvet's grip. "Asair!" she shouted. "Stop this now!"

She didn't understand. Dax squirming beneath him called to the magick craving revenge. "As much as I loved Elizabeth, Guardians should be killed at birth, as far as I'm concerned. You think you have so much control."

A few warbled words passed through Dax's lips, but Asair didn't want to hear excuses. He tightened his grip on his throat.

Dax kicked, jabbing his back with his knee. The pain cut, but he was done playing Guardian games. He loosened his fist, allowing the snake one last breath before he sucked the life out of him.

Natalie rushed into the room. She wheeled beside him, thrusting her hand out. "Stop! You can't hurt him. He's still connected to Halen."

Dax's face reddened, but Asair didn't budge.

"I can see her." Dax sputtered. "I can reach her seam." His gaze darted to Natalie. "I can bring her out."

Jae untangled herself from the tomb of fabric. "*Domolo*." She pointed her finger.

Asair skidded across the floor away from Dax. He hit the wall hard, the molding digging into his wounds.

"What's the matter with you?" She ran her hand over her bald head.

"We can't trust him." Asair winced with the pain.

"We don't have a choice," Natalie said.

"I don't want to die." Dax stood, smoothing his shirt over his stomach. "I didn't expect Huron would sacrifice me to Tarius. That was never the plan."

"You didn't think releasing a demon came with consequences? You're an idiot." Asair spat his words.

"Yeah, I am." Dax rubbed his throat.

"At least he's being honest for once," Natalie said.

"Honest!" Asair shot her a pointed stare. "You're not buying this, are you?"

"Just listen to him," Natalie said.

He turned to Dax, pumping his fists by his sides. "You manipulated Halen's magick—many lives were lost."

"Would you prefer I let her die? She never would have killed on her own. She needed a shove. I saved her life in the desert. I know what she needs. I'm her Guardian—not you."

Natalie wheeled beside Asair. "He's our best shot at bringing her out." She touched his arm, absorbing some of his rage.

His mind reeled with thoughts of Halen. "I'm not done with you." He pointed at Dax as he stepped around Natalie and stormed out of the room.

Jae followed him out of the room, her breath at his back.

"That moron can't bring her back. He thought by shoving her into the darkness, he was saving her. Thank heavens the owls hid the water stone, or he would have destroyed us all." Asair's voice rose with his frustration.

"We can use him," Jae said softly.

"Dax can't help Halen now." His sparks stirred once more with his frustration. He never should have left. Everyone here had gone mad. "He's pushed her too far. She's not innocent anymore, and Tarius will try to harness her dark powers. I don't how you could have let his happen."

Jae pinned him against the wall. "You need to pull yourself together. Blame will only fuel your rage, and when she brings Tarius out, he will use all our anger against us."

"What are you saying? She wouldn't bring him out. I know this about her. She would sooner rot in his hell than hurt any of us."

"She brought you out." Jae released her hold.

He pinched his eyes shut. "And she regretted it more than you'll ever know. She wouldn't make the same mistake twice."

"She doesn't have a choice," Jae said.

"What do you mean?"

"We're going to open the door." Her eyes gleamed.

He knew this look. This devilish stare that proceeded her sending a dragon to murder his Guardian. "I won't allow you to kill her." He pushed around her, stopping at the door where Halen's body lay.

"I would never hurt her." Jae's tone softened. "There's another way."

"Will it work?" His hand trembled on the doorknob.

"We have to try," she said.

He didn't hear doubt in her tone, but he felt it all the same.

"Calm yourself before you go in. Remember, her soul is out there."

When he opened the door, the scent of forest rain overwhelmed him. Water dripped from the ceiling, pooling in a basin and sliding back up a recycled fountain. In the center of the water lay the girl he had vowed to protect. Her skin was blotched black and blue with stitches across her cheek. He had failed miserably.

"What did you do to her?" He rushed toward her, only to be halted by the pressure of the water. "What is this?" He turned back to Jae.

"Just a spell I cast to keep her safe."

As he reached out, the force of the water shoved him back. "Remove it!" His voice cracked with tears. "Please."

"*Aquakiniumas.*" Jae waved and the water barrier collapsed to the floor, washing their feet.

He scooped Halen's limp body up into his arms. Her head lolled to the side, and he cradled the back of her neck, pushing her hair off her forehead. "I'm so sorry. I never should have left." He buried his head against her sticky flesh, the familiar scent of pine heavy on her skin— the scent of death. "You prepared her body for burial?"

"I only coated her in pine to preserve her body. Her magick is waning. We must reach her before it's too late." Jae placed her hand on his shoulder.

He leaned into her, tears shaking him as he rocked Halen.

"Dax has a way in," Jae said.

He brushed the tears from his face. "We can't trust him. Look at her. He's poisoned her with his darkness."

"My dear one, this is the only way. I've tried everything, but Tarius is strong. If she says the vows..." Jae sighed. "Once the words pass her lips, Tarius will have access to her soul. Galadia's fate was sealed many years ago."

"Galadia has lived many lives since then. Halen's soul is wise. She won't say the vows."

"She's just a girl."

"Halen's a blue moon siren. She has the powers of two realms. Have a little faith. She didn't let me take over when I was inside her. She resisted my charms."

Jae slipped her hand beneath Halen's head and gently guided her body away from him. "Tarius will come for the stone. We need to prepare."

"She won't say the words."

"When you were inside her, you saw everything. Every lifetime," Jae said.

He nodded.

"Then you know how much Galadia loved Tarius."

Again, he nodded. Her soul spent lifetimes searching for another bond like the one she had lost, always failing at matters of the heart and never finding the one she had loved more than Tarius. Perhaps forbidden love was the hardest for the heart to forget.

"Tarius needs her magick to touch the stone—all of it," Jae said. "Dax has seen her. She's confused. This is Tarius's charm. He's told her you're dead, but she doesn't believe it. She thinks Natalie is in danger. Tarius will use fear to control her. Dax is willing to help if we spare his life."

"No way. What happens after she's out? Already, Dax wants the water stone—he'll hand it right to Tarius."

Jae leaned in close. "Let me handle Dax."

He turned to read her face. From the years Quinn had spent with Jae, Asair knew from his memories exactly what she would do to Dax, and he couldn't be happier. "Fine. Let's bring her back. But if it doesn't work. I'll kill him myself."

"I'll prepare the others," Jae said. "I need to speak with Lina."

He kissed Halen's forehead, her skin cool against his lips. "Stay strong. We're coming for you."

26

ASAIR DOUBLE-CHECKED each lock on Dax's cage.

"This isn't necessary." Dax squirmed against the bindings.

"We can't have you running off to Tarius once he's out." He leaned against the cool metal, inches from the siren boy, fighting the urge to strike. He wondered if Jae had built the cage more to keep him from Dax. But as much as he wanted to tear him limb from limb, they needed the Guardian alive.

Natalie wheeled her chair beside him. "We're ready."

"Do you really think this will work?" Asair asked.

"I can get her out of Etlis!" Dax shouted.

"And you also admitted to leading her there." His grip tightened on the bars.

"Stand back." Lina rounded the cage. "He's no good to us dead." A cape the shade of the ocean in winter draped her shoulders. Her hair was adorned with little bones and periwinkle, her face washed in coral dust. She was dressed for war.

"When we're done. I'll let you have him." Vita entered the parking garage with Emil by her side. She tapped the hilts of blades at her waist. Emil tossed their bows and arrows into the back of the Escalade.

"I'm afraid I'll need some time with him first." Jae

headed toward them with Tasar. Tasar carried two leather cases, the glass bottles inside chiming with his lumbered gait.

"We made a deal," Dax said. "I lead Halen out and you spare my life."

"And we will all keep our promise." Jae turned away from him and winked at Asair.

Asair knew all too well there were far worse fates than death.

The sharp scent of pine filled the air and the elevator chimed. The doors parted and a collective gasp whispered their concern.

The two servers Asair had given his blood to guided Halen into the garage. She lay on a slab of marble. A sheet of fine chain-linked armor draped her body.

Asair clutched his chest as the marble floated past him and into the service van.

"Start the air conditioning." Jae wedged in beside Halen.

The engine roared to life and Tasar handed her the potion cases.

"It's time," Jae said, nodding. She smiled faintly and waved the doors shut.

Asair flinched with the sound. He wanted to be the one to go with Halen.

"Help me with him." Natalie tugged him back. She raised her hands and Dax's cage rattled.

Asair clasped her wrist. Their magick charged along his skin. Dax's cage drifted into the back of the second van. Tasar slammed the doors shut and joined his sister, who was in the SUV ahead.

Emil opened the passenger door for Natalie. He scooped her in his arms, holding her against his chest. She draped her arms around his neck, leaving a long, lingering kiss on his lips before he set her in the seat.

She could get in by herself, Asair knew, but after today, she might never have the chance to be in the Hunter's arms again. They weren't the only ones making a sacrifice. If Etlis opened, the Hunter's curse would break. Emil and Vita wouldn't come back to their home. If, however, they failed, it would be Asair and Natalie that didn't return.

MILES OF SAND stretched before them with a thin road that split the desert down the center. With each passing mile, Asair tuned out Natalie's aching heart and shoved his emotions deep inside as he listened for the call of the water stone.

Jae's plan ran through his mind; soon, she would stop Natalie and his heart from beating. With all three heart-beats silenced, the door to Etlis would split wide open. Once Halen reconnected with her magick, Jae would restart their hearts. Tarius didn't have a chance against three blue moon sirens and Galadia's wand. Only Asair knew from watching others' lives for a hundred years that no matter how good the plan, fate would bend to the heavens' will. He only hoped the heavens were on their side.

His sparks enlivened, the hairs on his arms rising. His ears rang with a familiar haunting song. "Stop the truck. It's here."

Emil cut the engine, and Asair hopped out of the SUV. He scanned the open desert, the heat roiling his insides. Though half of him belonged to Earth, his Elosian side craved the water. This was no place for a siren. The owls had been clever to hide the stone here.

Jae stepped from the van with the others by her side.

"This is where I felt it too," Jae said. "I think it's buried there." She pointed to a dip in the landscape.

Flattening his hand to the warm desert sand, the grains danced beneath his palm.

Natalie unrolled her window. "I hear it now. Let me out of the truck. I can find it."

"Shh." Asair walked a few yards away from them, their heartbeats and breath all a distraction. Connected in the circle of three, the pull of magick, like a thread stitched in his soul, tugged him toward Galadia's wand.

Drawn by a resonating hum, he titled his head to the ground, following as the vibration increased with each step. Slowly, the sand spun at his feet and with each step, the force increased. He yanked the yoke of his T-shirt up over his nose and shielded his eyes in the crook of his elbow as he pushed through the sand cloud.

Jae spoke words of magick, trying to part the grains, but no spell could stop the force as the stone called to his blue moon siren soul.

His skin prickled. "It's right under my feet."

"Are you sure?" Jae crouched beside him.

"Oh yeah, it's sparking my magick."

"Then this is where we do it." She clapped her hands.

"We should take the stone back to the fortress." Emil's gaze pinched with concern as he glanced back at the truck, where Natalie leaned out the open window. "If it's still in the car, then we can tow it."

"A few seconds." Jae placed her hand on his chest. "Natalie's heart will only stop beating for a few seconds. As soon as the portal to Etlis opens, I'll remove the spell."

"We're vulnerable in the open. If my brothers and sister come, they won't show mercy. This won't end well." Emil grasped the hilt of his dagger.

"I'll be by her side," Asair said.

"Your heart won't be beating either," Emil reminded him.

Lina coughed into her sleeve, clearing her throat before

speaking. "We have to do the spell here. Halen will need nature to fight Tarius. A blue moon siren harnesses their powers from the elements. Trapped inside a concrete barrier like your fortress will only weaken her. If Tarius claims her before we can unite her soul with her magick, then we will need all the help we can get from Mother Nature."

"Assemble the tents." Asair nodded to Jae. "Let's get started."

"Hold up, there's a car coming." Emil reached for his bow and withdrew an arrow.

The car pulled beside Natalie's SUV, and Emil released his arrow. The rod sailed through the air, puncturing the tire and sending the car skidding into the sand. Emil drew another arrow.

"Stop," Natalie shouted. "They're sirens."

Asair's heart raced. *Sirens.* Had they come for the stone? He ran with his hands thrust against the air, and when the driver opened the door, Asair shoved it closed.

The driver shot him a stern glare. The girl beside him opened her window and released a warbling cry. Her spell cut the air, sending Asair to the ground.

As he crawled to his feet, his sparks flared. He struck out, but Natalie blocked his blow, shoving his magick into the sand. The spot exploded with a rumbling burst. "Catch is with them," she shouted. "Stop!"

Asair lowered his hands. Emil, however, remained poised for battle, down on one knee, arrow nocked in his bow.

"It's all right." Natalie waved to the sirens.

Catch hugged his boney frame as he approached the Escalade, his eye twitching.

She opened the door, and he threw his arms around her.

Emil ran, kicking sand up with his boots. Asair

remained close to the Hunter's side while Tasar and Lina surrounded the sirens' car.

Five sirens were crammed in the Jetta. The driver was a young man with ruddy red hair and a muscular frame. And even though his arm had been amputated, he would be hard to take in a physical fight. His companions each bore scars of shifter torture.

The youngest, a boy with a gold eye, waved. "Hi." His voice shook. "We're here to help."

"We don't need your assistance." Asair clasped his fists to tame the stirring magick.

The boy tapped his gold eye with his nail. "You're going to need all the help you can get when the dragon stops your heart."

"Orca, shush," the girl said.

"No, he's right." Jae joined Asair. "You're an oracle?"

The boy nodded.

"Then you know what we must do," Jae said.

"I've seen it all." The sun shone within the boy's knowing eye. "There isn't much time."

27

Halen hadn't expected his idea of renewing their vows to include such a lavish celebration, but it was as if Tarius had a big stack of Martha Stewart magazines stashed away in Etlis and had taken tips from each one. A canopy of fire loomed below; the flames arrange so they appeared as brilliant, flickering flowers. An intricate pathway of ash spread along the ground with patterns of fish, seahorses, and coral blooms. Even with all the decay, Tarius invoked beauty, which only sickened her more. This opulent display was all for Galadia.

She turned to the dress spread across the altar; a gown of feathers and dragon sequin scales in pristine condition from years preserved in a crystal box of magick. As she picked up the gown, the scales shimmered in the glow of the fire. She ran her fingers along the sheen, thinking of Jae. What was she doing now? Was she mixing potions, searching her scrolls for a way to bring her back? Or was she preparing Natalie for an eternity inside the Hunter's gold arrow?

She only hoped she wasn't too late. She would need her sister on the other side. Halen would say the words Tarius wished to hear. After, all bets were off. She would rip his heart from his body, feed it to the desert sun, then turn the stone on his soul.

Halen stepped inside the gown, pulling the silver threaded fabric up her fragile body, thankful the length covered her ravaged legs. She fastened the little claw hooks which lined the front. Glancing in the mirror, she cringed at the apocalypse zombie prom queen staring back.

As she tucked a wisp of lavender hair behind her ear, her fingertips flickered with sparks. She stared at her hand with surprise. Her breath quickened as the skin healed along her arm. "No, no, no." Panic washed over her. This wasn't her body. Hers lay in Jae's quarters.

Her ears rang with the familiar hum of the water stone. Its low alto tones rolled through her. The vibration worked from her brain down to the tips of her toes. As the hum deepened, sparks trickled along her arms and legs and her bones coated with soft, new flesh. She yanked her sleeves down, not wanting to witness the transformation. If she healed in this body, would it trap her soul too?

Heart racing, she ran to the window where Tarius waited beneath the fiery canopy. A dragon swooped down, and as it landed next to Tarius, he transformed into the long muscular body of a man, his skin the color of midnight. She leaned forward, wishing she could hear their conversation. As if feeling her watchful eye, Tarius glanced toward the tower.

She backed away from the window, clutching her chest. She couldn't do this. *You need to buy more time.* She reminded herself. *The vows are nothing more than meaningless words.* But her heart said otherwise. These vows were sacred.

At one time, they had held great meaning. So much so that Tarius wanted nothing more than to hear them spoken once again. And an empty ache she tried to deny had filled her since he mentioned the vows. She couldn't say them.

The stone sang and she swallowed back her tears. If she could hear the water stone, then Natalie was already dead, and it meant that Tarius hadn't been lying about Asair either. She could never go back.

Your magick will save the realms. Her mother's soft voice filled the room.

Halen spun, searching. "Mom? Are you here?" She balled her hands into fists, frustrated Tarius had taken her life too. "Mom, I need you!" she shouted. "I can't do this alone."

A cool breeze rushed in from the window. She inhaled the vanilla scent, the familiar perfume of her mom.

You've never been alone. The winds whispered with her mother's voice.

Halen met her reflection. Sparks danced along her new flesh. She stared beyond the girl in the dress, searching deep inside for the reflection of her soul. In her eyes, she caught a glimmer of her true self. She smiled, knowing no matter what form she took, she always had the power.

And there were others who needed her. Even though the pain of Asair and Natalie's deaths stung, there was still Luke and the sirens, Catch, Lina, and Tasar… friends who would stand by her side to end Tarius. She just had to get out of Etlis.

Gathering up her gown, she rushed down the stairs. She had entered Etlis beyond the forest. That had to be the way out. Tarius, no doubt, would try to head her off, but already her magick surged. Her body strengthened, matching the sparks as her mother's words fueled her stride. She wasn't alone. She never had been.

At the bottom of the stairs, she ran the entire tower, finding each room as empty as the first, and without a window or door. The place where she thought she had entered was patched over with stone. But the masonry appeared to be centuries old and coated in soot. She sighed. Maybe this wasn't the spot at all.

Her breath ached in her fragile chest, and she leaned

against the wall. Her hands warmed with the stone, her sparks twitching. Turning, she placed both hands on the wall. The rocks vibrated at her fingertips. She shoved the force of her magick, and they crumbled to dust.

A sort of pride wound through her as she crawled through her newly made exit. "You can't keep me here." She shook her fist toward Tarius's flames. Her gown caught and she tugged, ripping the fabric as she toppled outside. She tore the hem, tossing it to the ground.

She turned to run when a portly hog cut her off. Halen flinched back as the ravaged beast snarled. Her eyes widened, taking in the grotesque animal. Its snout was black with soot, its ears crusted with blood. Along one side, skin curled back from the bone, revealing charred lungs through a broken rib cage.

She lifted her hand to strike, and the hog let out a shrill squeal.

"No, shush." She pleaded with the hog.

The bone hog shifted, its body slipping away to a portly young man. He stood before her; his frame stricken by years of flames.

She darted forward, but the boy grabbed her arm, yanking her back. His bone fingers cut into her flesh, shaking her hard. "You can't run from Tarius." His curious gaze drifted along her new, fleshed arm. "It's true." He tugged her harder.

Tarius rounded the corner. "Let her go. She's your queen."

The boy dropped his hand by his side, bowing his head, though his gaze never left her arm.

"Make yourself useful. Bring up the kwikilum. We will celebrate tonight." Tarius dismissed him with a wave.

The boy glanced back, and a smile filled his face as he disappeared around the corner.

"You tore your dress." The disappointment in Tarius's smoky voice gripped her attention.

He leaned against the tower. He wore a tuxedo of blood-red dragon scales, and atop his head sat a crown of crooked bones set with dazzling diamonds. The right side of his face, where she had torn his flesh, was now covered with an etched bronze metal plate, which contoured his cheekbones and wrapped under his chin, fastened to his jaw by a claw hook.

She tugged her sleeves down, not wanting him to see the work of her magick. How long she had been in Etlis, she didn't know, but she felt as if her body on the other side was running out of time. The more comfortable her sparks grew in this body, the more she feared they would nestle in like a corpse in a crypt, never to be seen on the other side again.

She clenched her fists. No way would she allow her magick to thrive here. She had a body to get back to—a home waiting for her—a life.

"It doesn't matter." He let out a heavy sigh. "We can get you a new dress when we leave here."

"You think a dress will make her happy? You know nothing about Galadia, then."

He snorted with laughter. "No, the dress is for me." His eyes gleamed with a sickening hunger.

Even though he terrified her, Halen had a slight advantage. His love for Galadia was his greatest weakness. He wouldn't harm her, otherwise, he wouldn't have a host for her soul. "I know you think this is the way but forcing me to renew some vows won't bring Galadia back."

"When you speak the words, her soul will remember. Think of your sister. She can live."

She didn't dare tell him the song of the water stone called to her. Her sister's soul was lost forever in a gold arrow. At least that's what she reasoned Natalie would have done once Asair died. "Natalie's soul is safe. She will never allow Dax to take her life. Didn't you know she loves a Hunter?"

He cocked his head to the side as he registered what she was saying.

"We could stay here for eternity," Halen called his bluff.

"She wouldn't allow a Hunter to capture her soul. The suffering would be immeasurable. Surely she would welcome a quick death at the hands of Dax."

"You don't know my sister." She smiled and his slipped from his face.

She had him.

"Doesn't matter." He shrugged. "Wherever we are, I welcome an eternity with you by my side."

"We won't last in these bodies."

He glanced skyward to the crying dragons. "We can be anything we want."

Did he really have powers this great? Jae mentioned Tarius had died long ago, and his soul could take any form he wished. The thought sickened her.

"Come, Darion is waiting for us." He headed toward the canopy of fire flowers.

Fearful of a fate inside a tortured dragon, she followed. Stepping away from the tower, a dragon swayed above, its scales glistening against the flaming sky. The heat caught in her lungs—lungs that were healing and dying over and over again with her magick.

A man with a bare chest, his muscles strong, the lower half of his body covered in scales, stood at the end of the grand canopy. Another stone altar sat before them. Tarius lay on one, beckoning her to lie beside him.

"No." Her voice was but a whisper, but Tarius waved her forward.

"No." She spoke louder.

"Galadia." He swung his legs over the stone slab and sat up. "Don't let this foolish Halen girl cloud your heart. Come to me." He reached for her hand.

She yanked away and as she did, her sleeve rose.

His face flickered with surprise. "Your magick is returning." His smile broadened. "So will your memory."

"Galadia." The Etlin bowed at the waist.

Lightning cracked overhead and the dragons howled.

"Say the vows now." Tarius cast his gaze toward the sky.

Halen followed his concerned stare. Above, indigo waves flooded the red sky, blowing the billowing smoke clouds away. Her magick spun with the cool air rushing in.

"Now!" Tarius wailed, the sound reverberating in her chest.

"Never." The wind called to her from within the blue sky, and the water stone sang out her name. "I will never say the words." This time, her voice spun, rising like a murder of crows screaming from deep inside. She cleared her throat, releasing the voice from her soul.

"Galadia, my love." He dropped to his knees.

"You betrayed the heavens' will." Her fists shook with her fury. "I could never love you." The air fell with a deathly chill.

"If you just say the words, you will remember how sweet it is to love one another again." He reached out for her.

The struggle tugged Halen inside out as her thoughts collided with her soul's remembrance. Life after life, she had fought to be free. Loving Tarius was her soul's greatest burden, and as she had tried to deny the love she harbored for this monster, never in all her lifetimes had she loved another more. She hated how a love so wrong could be so perfect.

"Say it." Tarius took both her hands in his. The winds

whipped away the flamed canopy, destroying the intricate ash artwork. "Please, my love, before it's too late."

Her memories flashed, and before her, a young man with waves of black hair stared back. She knew his locks were soft as new silk and smelled of summer clover, for she had nestled in the crook of his neck many times before, kissing his dark skin, which was always warm against hers —a shifter boy she had dared to love when the heavens had promised her to another. She had suffered a thousand lifetimes for this forbidden love.

"Please say the words." He kissed the tops of her hands.

Her pulse raced, igniting a new fire inside her—one brighter—one more powerful than all of Etlis's flames.

"*Tomlo*," Halen whispered.

28

TOMLO. The word felt so familiar on her tongue. She stroked his cheek, and Tarius's skin softened with new flesh. He smiled, his lips parting, and she guided him up, wanting to claim his kiss. "*Fikso,*" she said. This time, her voice was steady.

The winds whipped with a frosty chill as delicate snowflakes fell around them. Dragons cried overhead, but she could not tear her gaze away from the boy with soft eyes, snowflakes in his eyelashes, who had loved her for centuries. He had lost his way, but she could guide him back. "*Swa...*"

"You're almost there." His grip tightened.

Her eyes shut as a new surge of memories flooded her mind. Tarius stood on a mountain with the fire stone in his fist. The Etlins climbed toward him, only to be struck by flames. One by one, he slaughtered his children of Etlis, his rage destroying the beauty of the realm until nothing but bones and blood remained.

A flash cut through this memory and Halen found herself standing in a magnificent hall of amethyst; the floors, the ceiling, the walls all a brilliant hue of violet. At the end of the hall, two stones sat beneath a ray of light, and behind the wands stood Tarius. He reached for the stones and her eyelids shot open. She remembered every-thing, including his greatest betrayal of all.

"You stole the stones." She gasped for breath.

His face flickered with surprise. "You wanted to be together—forever. The stones were the only way."

"You never told them it was you."

"I did it for us."

"And they banished us." Halen recalled now the loneli-ness of the empty realm. Galadia's constant sorrow and regret. She had created Elosia out of remorse, her gift to the heavens, a plea for forgiveness. "I know why Galadia never wanted to see you again—she could never forgive you. You took away all she loved: her family, her friends, her home. She died hating you."

His gaze sharpened with anger.

She jerked away.

"You will say the words!" He stood, towering over her, but his gaze shifted to the forest.

Trees snapped, falling to dust as the horizon broke with a new landscape of warm golden sand. And a hum rever-berated through Etlis, rolling through Halen calling to her magick. The water stone was near.

Tarius spun into hooves and fur before she could blink, and he bounded for the desert.

She ran, but her feet were no match for the stag. When she waved, glistening feathers spread from her shoulder blades, elongating to wings, and her body transformed into an agile bird. She darted into the air, weaving in and out of the flames, chasing Tarius as he thundered toward the open desert spreading before them.

In the distance, she spotted three silhouettes draped in shimmering metal, lying side by side in the sand—Hunters' arrows aimed at their chests. Halen pushed harder, passing the stag. As she neared the bodies, she spotted her sister's dark hair spread along the sand, and next to her listless body—Asair.

Her thoughts raced; if the Hunters had arrows pointed at them, then her sister and Asair weren't dead. They had opened Etlis—they had a plan.

Halen beat her wings, calling the winds with her magick to propel her. She darted for Ezra, knowing Otho wouldn't spare her sister's soul. She pecked his head, cutting his scalp with her beak. He swatted her away with a heavy blow, and the gold arrow shot into the sky. She then darted for Aurelia, clipping her cheekbone with her wing.

"Stupid shifters!" Aurelia swatted Halen, but she dived before she made contact.

The other Hunter—she did not know this one by name —had the same thirst in his eyes as his brothers and sister, and he nocked a gold arrow and aimed for her. Magick wouldn't divert the power of the golden rod; she had tried and failed before.

She zigzagged, and he mimicked her every move, but before the arrow released, a growling beast leaped in the air, shoving the Hunter to the ground. Halen caught the gaze of her friend in the bear's eyes, but the reunion lasted for only a moment before Tasar turned and bounded across the sand toward the stag, where a geyser spurted from the desert and Lina stood on the edge, pulling the portal closed.

Jae transformed into claws and scales, her silver wings flashing against the sun. She hovered over the three bodies, then parting her jaws, she released a whooping cry. Glittering dust rained from her nostrils, falling all around them. Natalie rolled to her side, coughing. Jae drifted higher, then darted for the Hunter heading their way.

Halen fluttered over Asair, pecking at his hair, but he remained still as stone. *Wake up!* She wanted to scream, but only chirps escaped her throat. Her heart beat so fast she was sure it would burst through the bird's chest.

An arrow sailed past, and she turned to find Aurelia with a gold arrow nocked in her bow. So focused on a kill, the Huntress didn't even see Vita approach from behind. She twisted her dagger in her sister's shoulder, shoving her back with all her force.

Natalie peeled back the sheet covering Halen's body. "You have to connect now!" She shouted over the whirl of wind and sand.

Connect? Halen glanced at her body coated in a mesh pattern of Jae's sparkling dust.

"Now, Halen!" Natalie waved her hand, harnessing the wind and sand so they spiraled above her lifeless body. "Feel the magick!"

Halen dived into the current of her sister's spell, the sparks at once swirling around her feathers and together their magick twined, lacing in and out. She gasped as her soul pushed air into her lungs and her sparks ignited.

As her soul reconnected with the fibers of her body, her magick surged. She squeezed Asair's hand, forcing every part of her into him, working through his cells, his blood, winding her energy through to his soul. But still, she couldn't find him.

"Asair!" she screamed. "Come back to me!" Her toes caught, and when she glanced down, she found her toes tangled in threads; water washed over her feet.

Asair bobbed in a wooden boat, far out of her reach. She had found the seam of his soul, but they were not alone.

A boy stood in the shadows, smiling with victory.

"Dax! What are you doing here? You're not Asair's Guardian."

"When you shared your body with him, I learned the

way into Asair's seam. It's a fascinating place. You really should have a look around."

The sky churned with dark clouds. Asair clutched the sides of a boat bobbing in the dark water of his seam.

"Release him!" she shouted.

"Promise to protect me."

"I would never! You're a coward. And a murderer."

He shrugged. "And you're a puppet."

His words fueled her rage. She harnessed the water, cupping her hands, beckoning the boat to her. The wooden vessel fought the waves, while Dax stood with his arms crossed. A wave rolled over the boat. "Asair!"

"Halen!" Asair shouted over the howling wind. "You have to leave." He blew, so the boat drifted farther away, and when she opened her eyes, she found herself back in the desert, with Asair motionless by her side. She gathered him up by the shoulders, drawing him against her chest.

Natalie hovered in the air, her legs swaying in the turbulent desert winds now flowing from a water vortex spun by Lina. "Leave him. We need you." Natalie sailed toward the SUVs, where Tarius and Tasar battled.

Tasar struck the stag from the back, but Tarius bucked him off. The great bear twisted, bending. Each bone snapped, reverberating in her eardrum. She squinted when a sharp glare hit her sight. The rays bounced across Tasar's body, and when she focused, she found the source. Lacelle and Orca hid beneath the SUV, the young boy's eye shining. The bodies of Harry and Boris lay broken in the sand; a gold arrow stabbed Faisal's chest. She scanned the vast landscape for Luke, but it was Tarius who spotted him first.

Luke rushed him, but Tarius charged, pinning Luke to the SUV with his antlers.

"No!" Halen shouted, and the desert rose to her call. The sand spread and her mother's sedan rose out of the desert. The wand illuminated the interior with a brilliant glow as the stone cried out to Halen. Her hands throbbed, awaiting its power. She set Asair down, building a protective circle of sand around him.

As she made her way to the water stone, the ghosts of the slaughtered shifters and sirens twisted through her memories. Their blood called to her thirst for revenge. She waved, and the wand flew into her hand. Even in the heat of the desert, the wand warmed in her palm, the magick intertwining with hers.

"Tarius!" Her voice was thunder in a cloudless sky.

The stag turned, releasing Luke. Tarius struck the ground and the earth rumbled beneath Halen's feet.

She widened her stance to steady the raging force rising inside her. She clutched the stone, inhaling a deep breath. Her magick charged along her skin, ready to strike, but Tarius retreated, darting the opposite way. *What the hell?* He bolted toward the road, targeting a cargo van set apart from the SUVs.

"Halen!" Natalie shouted.

She turned as a Hunter bounded for her sister. She thrust the sand in front of Natalie, blocking the Hunter with a wall of sand.

Natalie flew up in the air, heading toward Tarius.

"Nat, stop!" Tarius didn't care what happened to Natalie. He would kill her without hesitation.

"Dax is in the van!" she shouted.

Her words slammed Halen like a tsunami hitting the shore. If Tarius reached Dax, then he could possess his body. He'd have control over her—Tarius would have the power of her magick and the stone.

She raised the wand, parting the sand, rushing Tarius. Her body ached with the heightened pressure as he opened the van doors.

Jae swooped from above, lifting the vehicle into the air and out of the stag's reach.

Tarius's spirit united with the sand before Halen's next breath. The grains spun, tearing up the desert. Halen shielded her eyes with the crook of her elbow, peeking as the sand elongated into the form of a golden dragon.

The sand dragon rose with fluid motion, striking Jae. As the van dropped, Tarius shifted the sand, cradling the van. But Jae struck him once more. The two rolled in the air, the sand binding and unbinding, as the dragons fought for space in the sky.

When Tarius slammed Jae to the ground, the water stone sung with a high-pitched squeal. She glanced to Lina's geyser sprouting from the desert. *Water.* She was half Elosian—water was hers to command. With a strike of the stone against the air, Halen called to the droplets, forcing them to spread.

Lina jumped back at once, spinning into her bird form as a wave crashed against the sand.

The saltwater intertwined with Halen's magick, and she tugged the geyser, stretching it wider until an ocean streamed across the desert.

Fighting the diminishing desert, Tarius gathered the sand, his dragon body growing in girth and strength.

Halen dived into the ocean, inhaling the saltwater, and pulled it deep into her chest. When she surfaced, she blew out with a forced breath. The water rushed the sand dragon, splitting the grains.

But Tarius was faster. He bounded for the desert, seeking more sand to rebuild his body. And his form strengthened with each breath.

Halen thrust through the current, charging him. At the base of his tail, she leaped onto the dragon's back. She ran up the sand scales while Tarius tried to shake her off. Grasping the beast's back, the sand glided through her fingers as she climbed. But she couldn't find her grip.

Striking his tail against the ground, the dragon tossed

her up and away from the water. She tumbled off, her skull hitting with a heavy thud, and the water stone rolled from her grip. Halen crawled toward the stone, inches within her grasp, but seeming miles away.

The dragon clawed her back, the weight of its foot shoving her deep into the desert earth.

The sand cascaded around her, sinking her farther and farther. "No!" she cried, reaching up to him. "Think of Galadia." She spat the sand from her mouth.

The dragon cocked its head to the side, its golden stare penetrating. "I don't need Galadia's love when hate feels this good." Tarius's low growl shook the ground. And the sand caved, the grains rushing all around her.

Halen clawed the sinking ground. Her energy waned as she searched for the stone. She held her breath fighting the suffocating sand. When she pushed the sand from her eyes that's when she spotted it; a blue sheen nestled near the crook of the dragon's tail. The water stone.

"You can't kill me. You need me!" Halen reached toward the stone, and it vibrated.

His gaze darted, following the motion. He blew the stone out of her reach. "Oh, I will have you. I will have every thought, every wish, every dream of yours. They will be mine to command. You will rule by my side." With a sweep of his wing, the van containing Dax appeared. With one swift bite, he sliced the roof, revealing the boy inside. "We will be as one."

"Halen, help!" Dax cried as Tarius plucked him out with his teeth. Dax dangled in the sand dragon's jaws.

No way would he be her master. No one controlled her. And no one would manipulate her magick ever again.

With her focus on the stone, she harnessed her sparks. She shook the ground, dragging the sand toward her until the stone slid within her grasp. When her fingertips brushed the crystal, the stone flew into her hand.

With Tarius focused on Dax, she crawled out of the sand trap. When she surfaced, she found her sister, both hands stretched outward, harnessing the water into a towering wall, keeping the shore at bay.

"Let it go!" She ran toward Natalie.

Natalie clenched her fists at once. The water wall collapsed, sliding over the desert.

Halen pulled the force of the ocean, using the water stone to guide the raging water toward Tarius. The wave slid up the dragon's tail, eating the sand scales away.

Tarius dropped Dax in the water and her Guardian dived, vanishing into the waves.

As the water swarmed the dragon, the sand fell flat. A stag now appeared before her, its grand antlers glowing bronze against the sunlight. Tarius shook the sand and water from his coat as he reached toward the sky. He pulled the clouds, turning her desert ocean into a turbulent storm.

A wave swept her under, but this element was not his to command—water belonged to her.

Raising the next wave, she rushed the stag, sweeping the power of the ocean beneath him and dragging him into her storm. His hooves clipped her side as he fought to keep his muzzle above the water. Throwing one arm over the other, she swam even though her ribs ached with the punch of his hooves.

As he drifted toward her, she waved the wand, summoning the water and pulling him under. When the tips of his antlers faded in the water, she dived. *We're not done*, she said, channeling her thoughts.

I wouldn't have it any other way. His voice filled her head. The water wound behind him, rising, coiling long with an undulating force until a serpent emerged. Its body swayed, preparing to strike.

Halen kicked back, shielding the stone against her chest.

The serpent's watery jaws spread, and it lunged.

Pinching her eyes shut, she dived between the pointed fangs. Halen thrust the wand outward, and the water crackled to ice. She blew all around, coating the serpent's insides with her magick, and with a crying wail, Tarius exploded.

She spiraled downward with the force of her magick as the infinite pieces of the serpent floated to the surface, melting in the warmth of the desert sun. The water stone hummed, fading to silence, and her hunger waned with the fullness of vengeance.

ASAIR WOKE to the tortured sobbing of a girl. Her sorrow twisted his gut. When he rolled to his side, he found Natalie clinging to Emil's body, or what little was left of the siren Hunter.

Emil shook in her grip, his skin withering to the bone. His legs jerked. His chest rose and fell with rapid breath.

Natalie thrust her hands against this chest and light burst from her palms. "No, no, no! Don't die on me. *Crysolo, malo, bastan!*" she shouted, but nature was deaf to her spells.

Emil's eyes rolled back in his head.

"Help me!" Her tear filled gaze met with Asair.

Asair placed his hand on her shoulder, forcing his magick through her to help bring the Hunter back. "What's happening to him?"

"The curse is broken." She sobbed. "The Hunter's lost their immortality. He's dying."

Asair scanned the desert, finding a vast ocean before him. To his right was a swirling orb where birds, coyotes, and desert shifters made their way through to the charred remains of Etlis. "Where is she? Where's Halen?" His fingertips sparked.

"Damn it." She shoved his hand off.

"Sorry." He shook his hands, now flowing with the full force of his powers. "Where is she?"

Emil gasped, lunging up for air.

"Help him," she called to Asair.

"I have to find Halen. There's nothing we can do for him now." Emil had helped him, but he had also killed many sirens over the years. Asair's loyalty belonged with his kind, not with a boy who should have died centuries ago.

"I need you." Natalie tugged his pant leg. "Please, just try."

Asair also understood the agony of death. Emil wouldn't be the one to suffer. His soul would move on, but Natalie would be left with the emptiness for the rest of her life. Grief always searched for a scapegoat; if he didn't try to help her, she would blame him.

He knelt, placing his hands on the Hunter's chest. He closed his eyes, searching now for an ember to fan.

Let me go. Emil's voice filled his mind. *There's nothing you can do.*

"Fight for this girl." Asair shoved his hands harder against Emil's heart.

We both know this is my fate.

A force shook Asair's hands, riding up his arms. He fell back against the sand, shaking his head.

"No! Try again!" Natalie cradled Emil.

Emil's skin peeled from his cheek. When the dry air touched the bone, the side of his face disintegrated into dust. "Rebuild Etlis, my love. Carry on my work."

"No, no, no. Don't you dare leave me," she cried, her tears falling in the hollows of his skull.

Emil transformed into bones in her arms, quickly crumbling and becoming one with the desert sand.

Asair turned away, her sadness too much to bear. He scanned the waves, inhaling the water, taking the power of the ocean deep in his breath, the taste of Halen's magick sharp on his tongue. He hated to think about what must have happened while he lay unconscious, and what still lay ahead. "I have to find her."

Natalie nodded, though she wouldn't meet his gaze. She cupped the dust of Emil's bones, trying to hold on to the remains of her love.

"I'll stay with her." Jae swooped down and landed beside him. When she shook her wings, the air cracked with her magick, and she stood before him once more in her human form. Lina and Tasar approached, with Ezra by their side.

"I'll go with you." Ezra bowed his head. With Otho no longer in control of his body, he had returned to the siren boy Halen was so fond of. "Let's go get Halen."

Glad for the help, Asair nodded. He admired Ezra for the sacrifice he made in the name of love. But he needed magick now. He needed Natalie, but when he glanced back to the shattered girl scooping sand into her pockets, he accepted Ezra's offer.

"If you encounter Tarius, stay back. He will need a host. A siren body would be perfect."

Lina leaned into her brother's side. Her legs were bloodied, her palms glowing a brilliant blue hue.

"You opened the portal to the ocean?" Asair asked.

"Halen needed the strength of water. It was the only way," Lina said.

He faced the waves, beating the newly formed desert shore. "She's in there." He whispered under his breath. "I can feel her." He turned to Ezra. "I'll handle Tarius. You get Halen out safely."

"She'll never leave you behind," Ezra said.

"She already has." Asair removed his shirt, his magick surging, ready for a fight.

Ezra pointed. "Wait—it's her."

Asair's sparks swelled as his gaze landed with Halen. Thick, inky sludge, the residue of dark magick and death, coated her body. He had witnessed demon possession before and knew better than to look hell in the eye, but he couldn't tear his gaze away from her. His magick skipped from one cell to the next, igniting in his veins as he tried to contain the urgency to strike.

Lina and Tasar both widened their stances while Jae gathered Natalie into her arms.

The sirens stepped from their car; their hands raised to cast spells.

Ezra shook his head. "What's wrong with you people?" He ran out to Halen, catching her as she stumbled into his arms. The water stone glowed from the crook of her arm.

"Get away from me." She raised her hand.

He gripped her wrist. "It's okay. The curse broke. I have my body back. You saved my soul." Ezra's smile reached his eyes.

"Ezra!" She stumbled against him, and he wrapped his arm around her waist. Her voice sounded the same, not a trace of hell. But they remained prepared to fight.

"Is he dead?" Ezra asked.

She nodded as he guided her out of the water. She glanced up, finding Asair.

"Asair!" She broke away from Ezra. The water stone slipped from her grip, landing in the sand. "I thought you were dead. I thought Dax had your soul." She folded into his arms.

"What are you talking about?" He held her back to gaze into her eyes. He looked from eye to eye, which were as green and bright as the day he had met her, not a trace of dark magick inside.

"What's wrong?" She clasped his shirt in her fists.

"Nothing. I'm just so glad to see you." He held her against his grateful heart.

"Asair!" Natalie shouted. And when he look over her hands were thrust toward the water.

Tasar shifted; the grand bear raised on his hind legs, releasing a thunderous roar.

Halen bent, clutching her chest. Asair's pulse raced as he turned to face the water.

Leathery stark bodies emerged from the waves. Rania stood in the center of her army, with Huron by her side. She shoved him forward as she strode from the water. When the beasts aimed their sickles, Asair nudged Halen behind him.

He lifted his hand to strike but felt nothing. He wriggled his fingers, he shook his fists, but it was as if the sparks had been stripped from his veins. A flash of a boy on his seam, the chains, and a boat plagued his mind.

"Do something!" Halen shouted.

He stared wide-eyed as Rania's army advanced. "I can't. My magick's gone."

30

WHY DID Dax still have a hold of Asair's magick? Surely, he didn't want to see them all die. Halen flicked her fingers, searching for her magick, but hers, too, fizzled. "Dax!"

She clutched the stone, and it hummed along her skin, awaiting her command. She understood the consequences, how if she harnessed the stone's strength as her own, she would have to give up a part of herself. But in this moment, surrounded by Rania's army, she had to protect the ones she loved. She was born with this power—light and dark—to save and to destroy. Inhaling a deep breath, she answered the call of the water stone—the call of her destiny.

Her sparks warmed, and she found her footing. Though Dax fought to hold her magick in his fist, she was stronger. He held the light, but the darkness was also hers to command.

She stepped around Asair, rolling her shoulders back. She thrust the stone toward Rania's army.

The savage beasts halted in unison.

"We mean you no harm." Rania shoved Huron toward her. "Take him as a peace offering."

Huron's terrified gaze snapped to Halen.

With the stone, she could see more clearly. Her father's

sins unfurling like her butterfly's wings before her. How Huron manipulated her mother into having a child; and how when she had twins, he had made her choose just one.

If not for her mother's cunning grace, he would have acted on her death sentence. *Murderer,* the stone whispered. His faults all lay before her, jagged rocks in her path. Each one cut more deeply. All he had ever wanted was her power. Even now, his greedy gaze fixed on the water stone, not his daughters. She would give him all he desired and more. She shifted the stone toward him.

He buckled to his knees. "Halen, no. Please." His mouth banded, crisscrossing with blood stained stitches.

She waved, and his body flattened to the sand. Her father's skin turned with a dark sheen and a tail sprouted from his back. His hands grew to pincers; his head sunk into his neck, contorting while it morphed into a tiny black speck.

The transformation lasted but a few seconds, but Halen would have enjoyed watching him writhe with the pain of mutating for hours. She couldn't recall a more pleasurable moment.

When no trace of skin or bone remained, she aimed for the scorpion.

"Enough." Asair guided her arm down.

She turned, cocking her head to the side. Asair's face blurred. His mouth opened and shut, but she didn't like the words tumbling from his lips. She tightened her grip on the wand.

"Halen. You need to come back to us." Natalie's voice rushed through her mind.

She blinked, spreading the fog, and bringing herself out of the stone's power.

Rania stepped back, commanding her army to lower their weapons. "The stone belongs in Elosia. Let us take it back." She nodded, and a Krull commander walked forward with a crystal box the color of a spring sky.

In her memories, Halen recalled the box crafted by a dear friend, the first of the Elosians to show her compassion and bring back the goddess she was born to be. Her friend understood the wand's thirst for power and how Galadia would bend to its desires. It took Galadia many years to wean herself from the stone's powers, but with guidance and love, she had found a way.

"Seal the box with Galadia's words." Rania nodded to the open box. "We will return the stone to Elosia where it belongs. No one,"—her gaze darted to the scorpion scuttling away—"will ever take it again."

"Promise no discourse between the realms," Jae said.

Rania bowed to the dragon. The movement was slight but coming from the warrior woman meant she would honor the agreement. "The war with the sirens will cease." Her gaze shifted to the water stone. "But you must return Galadia's wand to Elosia."

Halen backed away, the stone singing loudly in her ears.

"Let her take the stone." Jae nudged her toward Rania. "She cannot open the box. Only Galadia can touch it."

The stone warmed, sending a wave of sparks across her chest. She could leave with the wand, but she would have to fight. She turned, finding the siren boy, Luke. Fear flecked his eyes, and she didn't know if it was for the Krull or if his terror was directed at her. She had seen this look too many times—a look reserved for monsters. She didn't want to see it ever again.

Though the stone wailed with her decision, she waded into the water. When she placed the stone inside the cage, the wand squealed like an abandoned child. She blocked its cry, and with a wave of her hand, she spoke the words from her soul's remembrance, sealing the stone and its powers in the box.

"Thank you." Rania grasped her arm. "I will always do what is right for Elosia. The stone is safe. Elosia is your home, too. I see this now." Rania's gaze drifted to Asair. "My son always knew this. He sacrificed so much because he believed in you. When you are ready, I would like to show you Elosia. Maybe we can start over."

"I would like that. Thank you." Halen stepped away from the stone singing within the crystal walls, begging her to open the box.

Rania waved, and her army followed her into the ocean. They dived, and as the remaining Krull disappeared, Lina shoved the portal closed. The water spiraled, cinching until nothing but sand remained.

Halen leaned into Asair, her heart heavy, her body worn.

"You did it." He kissed her temple.

She didn't dare tell him the consequences of defeating Tarius, of harnessing the powers of the stone. Even with distance between her and the wand, the desire for blood pricked her skin. She bit her lip as Asair's pulse called to her hunger. Trembling, she shifted away.

He tugged her back, cupping her face in his hands. "What's wrong?"

She leaned into his warmth. "I feel so different."

"You're stronger." He pulled her against his chest.

"You're a badass, Mother Nature." Ezra stepped by her side.

"Amazing." Luke circled with the other sirens.

She met Luke's goofy grin, smiling, though inside, she fought the darkness spinning with her magick. The light seeming so far away. No matter the distance, she could not drown the song of the stone. She was one with its powers.

Not locked away in some crystal box beneath the waves. But finally free.

"Let's go home." Natalie took her hand, and her sparks quelled.

She looked at her sister, surprised by the calmness washing over her.

"I've got you." Natalie smiled.

"You feel it too?" Halen asked.

"It's nothing sisters can't handle."

"Sisters," she whispered. And she liked the way the word filled her with hope. Darkness may possess a part of her, but with Natalie by her side, it wouldn't win. "Let's go home."

ONE WEEK LATER

Firelight flickered along the shore, the embers drifting into the night sky like fireflies. As Natalie scattered the ashes of the one she loved into the ocean, Asair pulled Halen closer.

Once, Selene may have shed a tear at such a tender moment, but dark magick had stolen her compassion many moons ago. Now her heart beat only with the steady call of revenge.

"We should collect the ashes." Kye's fins swept the water, directing the current their way. "The ashes of the dead hold great power."

"No, sister." Selene smiled. "We have all we need." She pushed the damp hair away from the young man's face and over the antlers budding in his skull. Pressing her lips against his parted mouth, she inhaled his spirit, taking him deep inside. She jerked as the heavens and hell battled for his soul, but she would not let them claim him.

Not yet.

She fanned her tail, slowing the drift, inhaling every lifetime—capturing his sacred magick. When her lungs expanded with his soul, she let go, allowing the waves to bury his corpse.

Diya guided the Guardian boy's body into her arms.

Selene welcomed the listless boy, pulling him against her scaled chest. His birthmark glittered in the moonlight, sending chills of delight to the tips of her fins. With her sharp gaze fixed on the couple wrapped in an embrace on the beach, she exhaled, whispering against Dax's lips, "Breathe…"

THANK YOU

Thank you for reading *Smoke and Ruin!* It means so much that you took the time to dive into this world with me. Be sure to collect your free GUIDE TO THE REALMS. Keep the magick alive!

Tiffany

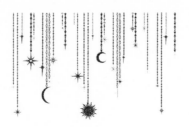

ACKNOWLEDGEMENTS

A heartfelt thank you to my editor Jill. I can't thank her enough for her dedication, encouragement and for pushing for excellence.

A very special thank you to Stefanie Saw for the stunning covers.

Hugs and thanks to my family of readers who are my everything. Thank you for your kind messages, fan art and for sharing your bookish love of the series.

And so much love to my husband and son for sharing me with the story and for their amazing support from the first word to the last.

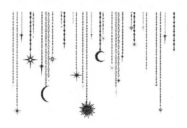

ABOUT THE AUTHOR

Tiffany Daune writes novels filled with modern magic, epic love, and dark creatures lurking in the shadows. Her young adult fantasy series, The Siren Chronicles, has been translated into multiple languages, as well as developed into an interactive game. Originally from Canada, she moved stateside, but never far from the water and draws from her scuba diving adventures for inspiration when building her fantastical worlds. She now calls British Columbia home and lives on an island with her husband and son surrounded by mermaids that are much nicer than the ones found in her books.

Visit her at www.tiffanydaune.com or anywhere online @Tiffany Daune.

Made in the USA
Coppell, TX
04 January 2022

70854115R00135